LAMBS OF MEN

Praise of *Lambs of Men*
BY Charles Dodd White

"Charles Dodd White has written this rich novel of the mountains as though he's been saving every word of it for a lifetime. A book full of beauty and blood and bone, a story that carries the reader through time, through lives, through dirt and fire."
—**Crystal Wilkinson**, author of *The Birds of Opulence*

"An elegant structure for a grim psalm."
—**Rob Neufeld**, *Asheville Citizen-Times*

More titles by Charles Dodd White

A Shelter of Others

In the House of Wilderness

How Fire Runs

A Year Without Months

Lambs of Men

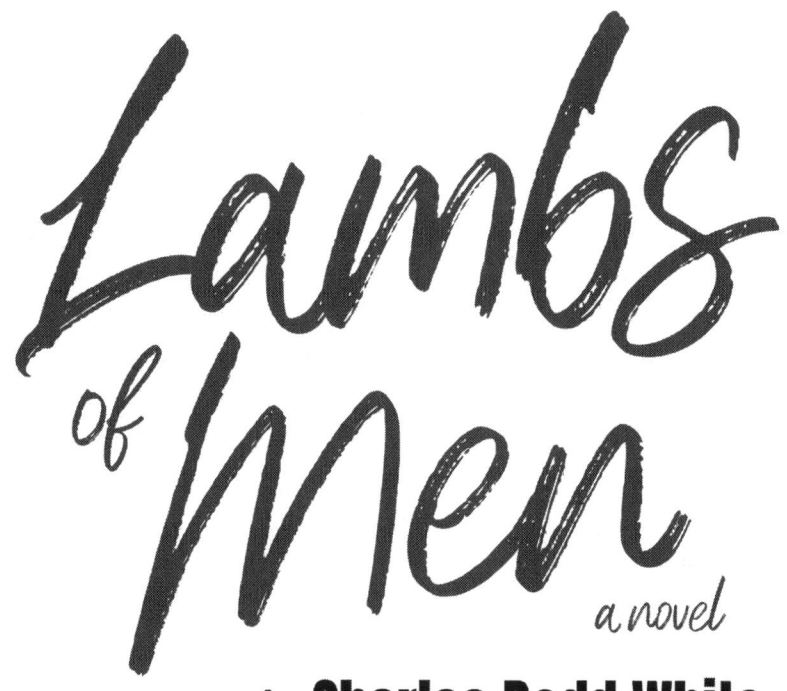

a novel

by Charles Dodd White

SHOTGUN HONEY

2022

LAMBS OF MEN
Text copyright © 2010, 2022 Charles Dodd White

All rights reserved. This book or any portion thereof may not be reproduced or used in any manner whatsoever without the express written permission of the publisher except for the use of brief quotations in a book review.

This book is a work of fiction. Names, characters, places, and incidents either are products of the author's imagination or are used fictitiously. Any resemblance to actual persons, living or dead, events, or locales is entirely coincidental.

Published by **Shotgun Honey Books**

215 Loma Road
Charleston, WV 25314
www.ShotgunHoney.com

Cover Design by Bad Fido.

First Printing 2022.

ISBN-10: 1-956957-08-1
ISBN-13: 978-1-956957-08-2

9 8 7 6 5 4 3 2   22 21 20 19 18 17

For Carl and Ethan White,
because men ask too much of their sons

Lambs of Men

Abraham took the wood for the burnt offering and placed it on his son Isaac, and he himself carried the fire and the knife. As the two of them went on together, Isaac spoke up and said to his father Abraham, "Father?"

"Yes, my son?" Abraham replied.

"The fire and wood are here," Isaac said, "but where is the lamb for the burnt offering?"

Abraham answered, "God Himself will provide the lamb for the burnt offering, my son." And the two of them went on together.

Genesis 22:6-8

One

1920

When there was no one awake but the sentries echoing slow steps across the floorboards of the squad bay, Hiram Tobit would sit at his desk in the duty hut still dressed in his sergeant's uniform. Sleep sometimes swooped in on him unawares, but never for long, and when the brief rest fled, he wondered if it had truly visited or he had given too much of himself over to waking dreams. It had been that way since he came back from the war in France.

He sat up full in his chair, stretching the muscles in his back and neck. His bones popped.

I'm nothing but an old skeleton.

He struck a match and lit the coal-oil lamp at the edge of his desk. With the wick turned up high, the pale diamond flame shivered up through the waisted globe. On the desktop sat a single manila file. He opened the front leaf and read the orders that he knew well enough to recite word for word. Home to the North Carolina mountains to recruit boys into the Marine Corps. Bring them in with promises and lies. He shoved the file back, his conscience itching. One thing to beat the hard sense of the world into boys as a drill instructor, another to hook them like bream.

He placed the campaign hat on his head and moved out into the squad bay. The sentry trotted up and reported the sleepers all secure in their racks. Hiram nodded and stepped outside, not interested in proper customs and courtesies at this hour.

The night was cool, the wrack of the marsh heavy. A chevron of geese cut noisily overhead as they passed across a gibbous moon. Hiram paused to gather their direction. Within a day or two they would cross the mountains where his mother lay buried. He knew he would be joining that course within the week: his first chance to see where his father had put her in the ground.

On his last afternoon on the island, he saddled up the gray gelding the command was giving him to travel his recruiting district. His mother would have approved. Him coming home like an old time Methodist circuit rider. He rode out past the rifle range with the February wind batting at his hat and the sun just beginning to set, the surge of the offshore breeze sharp. He rode through the sand and palms and stopped outside the whitewashed chapel where a flight of chimney swifts roosted in a dogwood tree, their bodies twitching in the branches.

His mother had always been fond of any kind of bird that flew in patterns. Said it was one of God's true wonders that a creature of boundless flight should seek the direction and comfort of its kin. Hiram didn't know if he agreed with that, but he was certain there were times when a man had to look deep into nature to remember where he stood in relation to it. He watched the birds for a long time and then rode back toward his duty hut. He needed to see that everything was ready for him to leave the next morning.

That night he dreamt of the war. Sometimes the visions came back in grotesque shapes that were but masks of the waking world. But this night memory returned as clear as a newsprint photograph.

The edge of Belleau Wood, France, in late May of 1918: the forest was a wall of scorched timber, ragged with stalks of smoke. Hiram's squad, just one of so many of the teeming Fourth Brigade, moved into the woods at regular intervals. The orders were to maintain silence, but none needed to hear that command repeated. Silence rose out of the earth in a fog that rubbed itself against any living thing. A voice was simply poisoned. The only thinly heard sounds were the slaps of rifle straps and the gritty crunch of deadfall beneath the men's shoes.

The Maxim machine guns opened up when the marines entered the valley. The whistling shot whipped down on them a split second before the report hammered through the forest. Dirt danced. Hiram deployed his men along a sunken road protected by the natural scoop of the hillside. The bullets carved air and slashed at the trees overhead. The incoming fire reminded him of being inside a sawmill.

He ordered his men to dig a hasty entrenchment along the muddy road while Platoon Sergeant Carson led the rest of the squad around an abandoned earthworks to probe for a possible flanking movement. Hiram's team returned the German machine gunfire, picking their targets carefully. He watched the woods down his gun sight for any brief muzzle flash. As soon as one appeared, he cradled the tip of his finger to the trigger and eased his breath away. The rifle jolted and then the flashes would stop. He chambered another round and waited, growing hungrier for each new opportunity to kill.

They moved through the woods, wriggling on their cold bellies and taking shots at the entrenched machine gunners. The platoon would have gone on but received the order to hold where they were or risk overrunning the advance.

The German infantry counterattacked the following morning at first light. They rushed like lunatics from the trees. Hiram fired first, crying out with a mad fear in the back of his throat that sounded like rage. The German infantry tried to push the assault but eventually melted back beyond the clearing, dragging their wounded behind. The dead remained.

They advanced and retreated and the days and nights swapped places, wrapped up in one another like smoke curling into the flames that generated it. Hiram and Carson and the rest of the platoon grew tired and hungry but they continued to push, driven by a need to remain in motion against the unnatural stillness of the forest.

On the fifth day, they took a heavy shelling. They fell in love with the earth, digging as far down as they could. They cast off their rifles as they flung dirt over their shoulders by the fistfuls. The shock of each impact made them shit their trousers until they had nothing more to void and they were left to wallow in their own reek. They cowered and wept while the barrage walked back and forth across their lines for most of an hour.

When the first of the marines broke and ran, Hiram knew it was only a matter of time before the others followed.

He backed them out as orderly as possible, withdrawing along the broad shoulders of a crater. When they had nearly cleared the area of impact, he heard a deep warble, almost a moan. He knew it was one of the ninety-five-pound shells fired from the big howitzers. He screamed for his men to seek cover, but before they could, the shell splintered an ash tree as big around as a boiler pipe.

The impact slung out a shower of tipped beams. The concussion of the explosion threw most of the men clear to the other side of a small ridge. But a boy named Givens was run through by one of the biggest splinters, pinning him straight through his gut to the ground. Sergeant Carson was the only man near him. He tried to work the splinter free, despite the man's screams, but the sharpened end was driven deep in the dirt and would not budge. The barrage intensified, and Hiram believed that the Germans were intent on pouring all of their evil into this one patch of the world. The ground liquefied. Carson's eyes took on a blind panic.

Givens reached out and gripped Carson by the wrist with iron fingers. Carson tried to wrench away, but the dying man would not release his hold. Carson kicked to escape, but still the hand would not let go. It happened very quickly, but even so, Hiram would remember it for the rest of his life. Carson clawed open his hip scabbard, drew his bayonet and began to hack away at Givens' arm. Why he didn't simply cut the dying man's throat, no one knew. Instead, he chopped into the buckling skin and bone while the dying boy's eyes walled like a horse.

Once clear of the artillery they scrambled back to higher ground. Along the way there were no sounds other than the hushed clattering of their equipment. That night, no one spoke above a whisper. Hiram tried to sleep but could only stare at the unstarred sky.

When he left the island the next morning, a warm front had moved in and the fog lay heavy over the sound so that when he led the gray horse onto the ferry, it looked as though he had dragged along a piece of animate and rebellious weather as his lone companion. The animal stamped and nickered, afraid of the same air it snorted.

"Shut up." Hiram pulled down hard on the bridle. Once the animal quieted he struck a match three times in the damp before it flared and he lit a cigarette.

The ferryman turned his head over his shoulder. "You might try talking sweet to it."

Hiram looked at him. "I might."

The deck moved under them, the hull slipping through the slack water like a chilled kiss. The old man had a way of not talking that made him seem hurt.

"How long you been ferrying?" Hiram asked.

"Twenty-five years, I reckon. When the Marines moved in in '91. I guess it's about that. What year is it now?"

Hiram laughed quietly. "You mean to tell you don't know the year?"

"Naw. I never took much account of the calendar."

"Well, I guess twenty-five years is close enough, then."

The old man nodded, studying the fog he piloted through. "Twenty-five years is an awful long time standing. If I had my count of boys younger than you I've hauled crossed this water in that time, it would be something else."

"How many, you figure?"

The old man stared dead on, seeing shapes out there

Hiram did not. "Well, as I said, I ain't no man of accounts. I don't know that numbers would tell what I've reckoned. What other things has I seen in that number to compare?"

"Not many, I suppose."

"No, not many. I did dream them once, though. Each blessed one of them, saw their faces just as clear as I see yours. They was strung out on the far bank standing next to one another, not saying a word, just waiting for me to carry them over to the island. I would take on as many as I could and try to catch the tide, but sometimes I would have to wait and that was the worst part 'cause they just stood there looking across the water at something I couldn't see. I began working faster to try to get them over, just so I could be shed of them. But the more I crossed over, the more that kept coming down to the far bank. The whole country had bust a dam and instead of water it was pouring out all its boys wanting to be soldiers. In time they weren't no room on the bank and they started walking down into the water until it closed over they heads and they drowned. But still them boys kept coming until the next ones drowned too and more of them still until they was enough dead boys down there for the new ones to stand on they backs without getting they shoes wet."

The old man was quiet for a long time before he spoke again. "What do you make of a dream like that?"

"I don't figure I can make anything of it. That's something else."

The ferryman nodded, distraction blunting the cut of his eyes. "You wouldn't have one of them cigarettes I could borrow, would you?"

Hiram passed the ferryman a cigarette and together they

smoked, watching where the sound met the banked air, listening to water rending beneath the ferry's bows.

When they reached the jetty Hiram led the shying horse out of the gangway and over the slick planks and dropped the looped reins over one of the bollards while he dug out the coin for his passage and carried it to the ferryman. He held the money out to him, but the old man waved it away. "You paid it already, friend."

"Why, hell. That cigarette didn't cost me nothing."

"I ain't talking about the cigarette," the old man said as he cast off to make headway on the turning tide.

By midday, he had come onto a wind-scoured road trafficked with every sort of commotion bound in or out of the Carolina Lowcountry. Even the occasional Model T truck gave a cheeky honk as it flew by, raising small whirlwinds of dust. The daily mania of commerce in the vicinity of Beaufort was a stark contrast to the regimented order of a training day on the island. Here, men and women in sundry raced along the road, their colorful clothing whipped by the breeze. The variety was something of a poke in the eyeballs for Hiram, having been for so long accustomed to a shallowly deviating hue of green.

He turned down Depot Road, passing a few haggard mansions with their diminished plantations reaching back into the cane-choked bottomland. Some were immense and impressive, but to Hiram they seemed more like museums, preserving a specimen of living that no longer bore a claim. He rode past.

He had nearly an hour before the train was due to leave. He stood on the platform holding the gray horse, watching the few men in business suits who watched him. It made him angry. A stranger's eyes were no better than rifle bores. They never simply looked on. They wanted something more, some clue or detail of the man inside, a betrayal of outward appearances. Men who wore expensive suits enjoyed pretending their place in the world was justified, earned, not a pitiless spin of the roulette wheel. So they carefully styled themselves, cultivated their false humility and bedrock arrogance.

He approached a circle of fellow marines waiting to embark. They stood smoking at the far end of the platform. None were familiar, but still they welcomed him. He didn't care, as long as he was among his kind. They asked him about the horse and tried to pat it along the withers, but the horse tossed its head and nickered and they stopped. Only two of the marines were veterans. The others, all privates, were going along the rail as far as Columbia on their way home on leave and were anxious to hear stories of the Fourth Brigade they could tell their friends. They admired the ribbons hung above Hiram's heart with faces broad and smooth, unscored.

Hiram turned to one of the veterans. "What is it with all these young sons, always wanting to hear stories about killing?"

The veteran laughed down at his shoes and stamped his cigarette butt. "They think it's how you get to be a hero."

Hiram shook his head. "There were a mighty lot of heroes over there," he said. "They've got nice little crosses above their heads to prove it."

The boys tried to laugh, but after that no one again mentioned anything about the war.

Two

When the train began its long climb, Hiram's heart fired a bolt and his guts drew small. The feel of the land rising beneath him touched memories he'd thought banished and now his remembering became an unstrung weight in his body. He leaned as far from the open car as he could to meet the down rush of chilling wind sharpened by the forward surge of the train.

The porter approached. "You can't do that, Old Sarge." He was tall and thin with an overcoat buttoned to the top of his throat and a wool scarf wound to the bottom of his chapped ears. "We can't have you leaning out of the windows like that. Otherwise we'd be liable for having your head swapt off."

Hiram crossed the narrow aisle to watch the horizon from the safety of the canvas-covered seats. The porter stamped up and down, his hands hidden in his deep pockets, talking with no one else because every other passenger had preferred the warmth and comfort of the enclosed compartments just forward.

"You want a blanket or something?"

Hiram only glanced at him. "Naw, I got a furnace in my belly. Don't ever get cold."

"What about a cup of coffee? Some oil for that furnace of youren."

"Now, I wouldn't be offended by that."

The porter smiled and went to fetch the coffee.

While he waited, Hiram smoked and thought about the many times he'd wanted nothing more than to get beyond this very country, about how he'd transformed it in his mind into a place that bore no claim on his sympathies. But he now saw how hard on his home he had been. Here, in the long, chattering climb up the grade, he recognized the overlooked details of what he'd mistakenly scorned. It wasn't the land he hated. It wasn't even the men and women themselves. What had hold of him had more to do with the past than the land. But he knew how easy it was to confuse the two.

The porter returned with two large pewter tankards capped with steam.

"Mighty generous of you."

"Sure. I couldn't have my only passenger turning up with pneumonia. How's that horse of yours fixed back there in the stable car. You need me to check on him?"

"He's fine, I figure."

"He's your horse, I guess."

The train drew them on into a russet valley that shut off their view of the distant range and gathered them into the shaded dimensions of the mountain country itself, the railroad tracks' right of way turning to ash. Hiram drank his coffee down to the dregs.

After the train leveled off, the sky lowered and the long

slate overhead began dribbling flakes of snow the size of pennies. In an hour's time it had grown dark and the winter crust lay like silence made visible over the earth. Another few minutes of rolling through the whitened dark and the engine reduced its power and the train braked with a great grinding sigh outside of an empty platform. A placard reading "Sanction" moaned in the wind.

"Any dunnage I don't know about?"

"Everything's back in the stable car. I can get it." Hiram counted out some change for the porter's services and made his way to the rear cars to bring down the horse. The beast was calm in its stall and remained so once saddled and bridled. He walked it onto the platform and watched the train put itself in slow motion and draw away to the fine, cowlicked bend in the track a quarter of a mile distant before he lead the horse down the station ramp and onto the slung gravel and blackened snow.

He paused there, watching the trees under their dusting, not sure what to make of his own arrival. He had expected no reception, no notice. Preferred it that way, in fact. But the stark emptiness of being alone in a familiar place touched him with a hurt he'd not expected. He talked to the horse for a moment, making with it a contract that he would commit no violence against the creature if it agreed to the same. He carefully drew his foot to the stirrup and gained the saddle. The horse did not offer complaint. Hiram clicked his tongue and pressed his knees and they were once more moving toward their destination.

The track they followed had been riven by long autumn rains and baked over with a winter sun, so that the ruts were deep and hazardous in the low light and fresh snow. Hiram let the horse move slow, feeling its way on the clay while he nodded in a half sleep.

When he woke sometime later they had come into a cluster of outbuildings, the remnants of an abandoned smithy. The workshop was dilapidated and the main building had fallen victim to scavengers at large, the front door absent from its hinges and pieces of clapboard pried clean away in places so that the moonlight shone through to the other side. Hiram knew he hadn't come far and that his sleeplessness, for once, was not reliable. He dismounted and tied the horse outside, putting him under a canvas blanket. He dragged the saddle in the building and found a beaten place on the floor that he kicked in, breaking the dried pine boards free. The fire he built shook warm colors on the rotten walls and ceiling; the thin, chalky smoke vented through the perforated roof. He wadded his greatcoat for a pillow and lay down beside the snapping fire. Before he knew he meant to, he slept.

He rose late to find the morning sun had already drilled muddy holes in the snow. He stood in the doorway looking at the horse while he smoked a cigarette and coughed.

"I guess you're about as ready as I am."

The horse said nothing back.

After a cold breakfast he rode up along an old timber mill clearing and past a few homeplaces with men who lifted their hands in passing welcome, acquaintances from years ago who might have recognized the phantom of the boy in the man's face. Hiram nodded as he met these men, but he did not stop nor shout hello.

The next morning he came to Henry's place with the cold

sun just risen. The dogs stayed clear of the horse, but once Hiram dismounted and came up to the house they were at him, snouting at his boots and hands, lapping their big tongues against his fist. He spoke their names and talked to them in a voice used only for children and creatures until they fell in step, walking at his side with a toss of their heads and switching tails, as if they were responsible for bringing this great wonder to their stead.

"I see they ain't forgot your smell."

Henry's mother stood on the porch. She held a black skillet as big as an empty belly. Hiram could smell the bacon newly fried.

"I guess I've still got the old stink on me, then."

She smiled. "Take that horse around back. I just might be able to find a place at the table for you."

Hiram said that he would be pleased to and led the horse into an empty stall, rubbed it down and came back to the front, wiping his boots on the sharp edge of a quartz-etched stone before he mounted the stairs and walked on into the house. Mrs. Buchanan had already set the plates out on the counter—only three. He knew what that meant.

"Mr. Buchanan?"

"Last spring, nearly a year ago."

Hiram tugged at the brim of his hat. "I'm mighty sorry for not knowing."

She reached out and touched him on the shoulder. "Lord, Hiram, we all knew it was coming. It was just a matter of when. I think he hung on those last couple of years for Henry's sake anyhow."

"Your husband was a mighty good man."

"He was that." She set a basket of warm biscuits in the center of the table and arranged three silver spoons fanwise for butter and preserves. "Why don't you go get Henry up? He won't even budge for me."

He moved back through the long hall, picking up his canine escort once more, and came to the shut door at the far end. He stood there a minute before he rapped three times hard on the panel and received no answer. The dogs snuffled against the doorknob, rattling it softly in its mounting. He knocked again.

"I'll be up in a bit, Mama."

Hiram repeated the three sharp knocks.

"Damn, I said I was comin'."

"This ain't your mama, soldier. This is reveille."

"Who in the hell?"

Hiram opened the door on his friend. Henry jerked up in the bed with frazzled sandy hair standing like the bristles of a riled wolf. It took only a moment to call his friend's name and great smiles wrecked both their faces.

"You've gotten lazy."

"Sure. That's one of the snares of civilian living."

He studied Hiram's military uniform. "I see you ain't given up the service."

"No, but it's 'bout given up on me. Hell, enough time for chatter. Your mama's got some hot breakfast in there for us. Let's get going."

Hiram knew what he would see next. He had heard what had happened from his mother in one of her last letters to him, had seen similar things to men in his own battalion, but when Henry whipped off his blanket and swung himself from his place on the bed down to the puncheon floor and slammed his calloused fists down like a pair of mallets, swinging his torso and what few inches remained of his legs in a seesawing motion, Hiram had to look away.

Henry glanced over his shoulder. "You coming?"

Hiram felt his voice thicken. "Yeah, I'm coming."

By the time Hiram went into the kitchen, Henry had already climbed up into his chair at the head of the table and was drinking a cup of coffee his mother had set before him, the ropey muscles in his forearms alive and serpentine even when at rest. Hiram sat down and Mrs. Buchanan set all of their plates. Then she laid her hands on both their shoulders while she remained standing and said the blessing over them both. Neither Hiram nor Henry chorused her Amen.

"When'd you get in?" Henry asked.

"Yesterday. By way of the Sanction rail stop."

"That's a good ride."

"It is."

Mrs. Buchanan leaned in. "How's your daddy, Hiram? I'm sorry to say I haven't kept up with him since your mama's passing."

"He's fine, I guess. I haven't been up to see him. Hadn't had time as of yet."

Henry and his mother exchanged a look. "Tell him I asked," she said.

"I will."

Henry cleared his throat. "You aim to get your own place, then, instead of staying with your daddy?"

Hiram swiped a wedge of butter across his toast. "Yeah. Probably lease me a place out from one of the storekeeps in Canon City."

Henry laughed, shaping his mouth carefully around the rim of his coffee cup. "That's a mighty broad sweep between here and Canon City. You must aim on being a wandering soul."

"It's what they've got me up here for. The Marines, I

mean. I'm the new district recruiter. Here to bring in all the squirrel-shooting hillbillies."

Henry roared with laughter and thumped the table with his palm. "Well, good luck is all I can say. Anybody wearing a uniform of the United States government up here ain't exactly the most popular feller right now."

Hiram smiled. "I'm not sure they ever were."

They fell to their meal with no more talk of the service or family and enjoyed the simple pleasure of being in one another's company after so long. Once they had finished eating, Mrs. Buchanan cleared the table and encouraged them to take their conversation onto the porch to enjoy the warming weather.

The two men took her suggestion to sun themselves out front while they watched the dripping thaw and listened to a flock of wild turkey cluck and scratch at the wet leaves just beyond the tree line. Henry's mother brought them out a steel pot of fresh coffee and slipped back inside without a word. They continued talking until midday when they decided to ride down to Lincoln Township to see what trouble might be found there. Hiram hitched an old buckboard to the gray horse, who stamped and shivered when married to the wheeled contraption but got used to it readily enough. Hiram unwrapped the trace chains from the brake lever and trotted the horse on out. Henry jostled beside him on the narrow seat, his strong fingers hooked on tight to the beveled edge.

They rode down the old trace through the second growth forest, the tall trees sketching lean shadows on the ground where streaks of vanishing snow still lingered. They stopped at a dogleg when they saw fresh sign of bear and discussed the likely business of that creature in that place and his direction of movement.

"Your daddy will want to see you, Hiram."

"Yeah, I know it."

"What you intend to do about it, then? It's been years since you left. You can't hate the man forever. What happened with Kite was done long time before you ever had a say in anything. Your brother died because of a fool accident. That's all it is. All it ever was."

"Is that a fact, now?"

"It is. There's no joy in it. Besides, you'll want to see your momma."

"Nothing to see but a covered hole in the ground."

"It's more than that."

"Well, Daddy's already managed to hide one grave up there. I don't doubt he would do it again."

"Just think on it."

"I've never stopped, Henry."

They continued on, riding down the gentle slope until they came into the first proper clearings of the hamlet.

They passed only a few men on the square as they rode up to the store and Hiram sat holding the driving reins while Henry monkey-climbed his way from the runner and propelled himself through the front doorway with the smash of his shoulder against the swinging board. When he came back a minute later, he gained his place on the seat and had Hiram put the horse in motion. They rode on through the square without stopping again.

"I'm gonna take you up to my wife's place. She'll set us up right."

Hiram studied his friend for signs of a prank but saw nothing. He was curious to see what such talk was about.

They found the peat house at the base of a hillock under several hairy cedars and a few big maples naked for the winter. Its roof was not more than seven feet from main beam to earthen foundation. A single window was shuttered with an age-faded strip of bark, allowing sight of the faintest glimmer of lantern light within, a humble yet hospitable abode, not dragged violently out of conflict with the elements of the natural world but in agreement with it.

Henry swung down to the ground as soon as Hiram put the horse to rest and beat on the little door. There was no answer.

"Atlanta, dammit! Drag your hide outta bed." He yanked at the door but found it locked. He thumped his fist against the bark once more.

"Maybe she ain't home," Hiram offered.

"She's home, all right. Atlanta!"

Even from where he sat, Hiram could hear sounds of movement inside, the shuffle of feet heavy on the packed dirt floor. A latch was thrown and the doorway suddenly filled with an image of exasperated womanhood. She was big with hair the color of brick and a complexion only one roseate hue removed. Even from a distance her appearance was tinged with a furious and implacable heat, like an electrical storm or a heart about to explode. Her wild hair grazed the lintel post of the little door even though she had stooped in order to look Henry in the eye, making her a good six feet, if not an inch or two taller. She wore only the flannel sheet of her bedding, wrapped around her vast humanity like a toga.

Hiram, rooted to his seat in the wagon, watched the pair with undisguised amazement.

Atlanta stabbed him with a dark glare. "Who in the hell

is he? I told you, Henry, I don't want you bringing your drunk friends up around here. This is my house, you understand? My house!"

Henry, his rancor crumbling in the face of his sweetheart's rage, drew his hand to her waist and let it rest there against her soft belly as he spoke words of supplication and tenderness. Hiram realized only then that Atlanta was pregnant.

After a few minutes of Henry's efforts at reconciliation, Hiram was allowed to come down and receive introduction. Atlanta shook his hand like a man and watched him with her fists on her hips. "You in the army with Henry?"

"No ma'am. He went up with the Canadians before I was old enough to join. Henry here's the one who taught me to hunt."

"Well, I guess you'd be wanting to sit down for a spell."

"I wouldn't mind it, no ma'am."

On entering the earthen house, Hiram was commanded to remove his shoes. He did so. Though the interior was small, the few chairs and tables were placed to allow an ease of movement throughout and Henry and Hiram were made comfortable in a pair of rocking chairs padded with down-filled cushions. They passed a few minutes in one another's solitary company while Atlanta busied herself with some preparation in the backroom.

"Your mama know about this wife business?"

Henry gawked. "Hell, no. She'd have me run off to the crazy house if she did. Either that or have the preacher come and try to save me all over again."

"That's a pretty big secret to keep."

"Well, I've managed to keep it fine, so don't go running your mouth."

"I didn't say I was going to say anything."

"Well, fine then. Don't."

When Atlanta returned, she held a pair of cob pipes. She handed one to Hiram and the other to Henry and lit them both. The smoke was strong and sweet in the confines of the small room and after a few puffs Hiram felt like he was plummeting through the peat walls behind him, his skeleton coming loose in the space between where he sat in the chair and where he felt his presence peeling toward the earth. He turned his head and looked at Henry who smiled and nodded, his eyes heavily lidded and subdued.

"My Atlanta takes care of me."

Hiram continued smoking, fastening his eyes to the oval rug at his feet with its intricate and writhing loops. Atlanta sat drinking a small cup of spicebush tea.

"So you come up here in that suit to drag other boys off, I guess."

It took Hiram a moment to realize he was being addressed. He tried to shape his mouth with some words, but the greater his attempts the more distant the prospect of language became. He managed only an effortful stare.

"Man like you was the one who got my brother sent off to the war. Didn't even get half a dozen letters from him before he was dead. Shot by some German sniper in a place he couldn't pronounce."

Hiram coughed. "I'm sorry to hear that." He wanted to be away from these constrictive surroundings. The smoke closed around him like a giant white snake.

"Yeah, it was sorry all right." She stood and went back to the kitchen and in a minute returned with a mug of the tea. "Here, drink it. It'll clear your head."

He took it and did as she said and within a few minutes

he sensed the ground stiffening beneath his feet and his body returning to itself, the illusion of his soul and body coming apart exchanged for the illusion of his body and soul made whole.

He looked at Henry who contentedly snored in a patch of dingy lantern light. "Do you really love him? Like he is now. All broken up."

Atlanta gutted him with her eyes. "Don't you ask me that, ever. Now, when he's fit, make sure you take him on home. His momma will be worried."

Late that afternoon, Hiram and Henry began the long ride back to Mrs. Buchanan's house with a cold wind coming off the mountain tops crowned with Canadian firs, the spired trees growing indigo in the winter sunset. At twilight they watched a herd of does moving along a ridgeline paralleling the causeway, the deer's breath visible in the air as a smoky chain loosed on the last faded illumination of the day already gone. They talked about the beauty of such a sight and afterwards rode through the darkness while Hiram silently remembered how many wonders and horrors he and his friend had seen and learned to accept in what were still such young lives. He knew there was something tragic in having been asked so much by life so soon, but he supposed they were not alone in this. From what Hiram had seen, men were doomed to repeat the sins of not only their fathers, but all their ancient forebears on back to Cain. That was the true mark upon man, scripted in his very blood.

When they came into the yard late and put the horse up for the night, they were careful to bed down quietly so that they would not disturb Henry's mother with any sounds that might give her alarm. Hiram stretched out on the hard floor at the foot of Henry's bed and they both sat up listening to a screech owl nearby, whispering about hunting trips they remembered from years past on nights not unlike this one. Then the owl ceased its call. They both caught their breath and strained to hear, as if guarding their souls from whatever predator could silence one of its own.

Hiram rode out the next morning, letting the horse pick his own way off the mountain. In so doing, he came down into the great valley where he was sure to meet the causeway in no time at all. The sun played at odds with the storm clouds all day long, intermittently baking and chilling as the scaling light pinned deep, definite shadows across the road. Hiram ate his lunch in the saddle, watching the few songbirds that braved the conditions while the land opened up. A hard storm came, but there was no shelter to be had on the open road. He held out his canteen cup to the downpour and filled it and drank while the water sluiced down his hat and the nape of his neck.

That afternoon he began to meet other travelers on the road. He knew he was closing on the county seat of Canon City and even a day as foul as this could not foreshorten all the assorted business headed in that direction. After the rain stopped, he entered the town at dusk under a freezing and welted sky. He was soaked through and though his uniform kept him warm, he was eager to stop at the first place he saw that advertised rooms, a gray clapboard two-story with windows dimmed by lantern smudges.

The woman, who introduced herself simply as the widow Stark, took his money and said it would be more than the normal quarter a night if they were to put up the horse and provide Hiram a hot meal. He paid her without complaint and handed the reins to a youth of about fourteen he took to be the woman's son.

The chamber he was led to was smallish, covered in a dingy arabesque wallpaper that swelled and drew around the irregular lumps and cracks in the plaster wall. The casement windows faced a backyard enclosed with chicken wire and inhabited by the drabbest looking collection of hens ever come to creation. He stripped out of his uniform and draped it carefully over the radiator to dry, the room quickly filling with the reek of wet wool. He stood naked in the center of the room, letting the moisture evaporate from his skin in the close heat. Once he was dry, he dressed in his only civilian clothing, a pair of black trousers and a matching pullover sweater.

After drawing his boots back on, he clumped down the staircase to a dining room near the back of the house where he could smell the evening meal. He stopped just outside and peered around the corner, not wanting to blunder in uninvited.

The widow Stark looked down from her place at the head of the empty table. "Get yourself a seat, Mr. Tobit. It's none but yourself and Albert that will be in this evening."

Hiram took the only place where china had been set, at the corner most removed from where the widow presided.

She made a deliberate study of him. "How long you been out there riding in that mess?"

"Since daybreak."

"I ain't seen weather the likes of that in an age. You musta had a reason driving you."

"No, ma'am. I just didn't have cause to stop."

"You aren't a deserter, are you?"

Hiram smiled. "No ma'am. I'm no deserter."

She sniffed noncommittally and drank tea from a tiny porcelain cup. "My daddy shot a boy who tried to desert General Lee's army during the war. Little son of a gun was hiding in the corncrib one morning and liked to have scared my momma to death when he shot outta there like some jack-of-the-box. It made Daddy so mad to have worked so hard, and him with only the one good arm, and to have this little scarecrow come along and pirate his stores. The little feller was lucky it was only bird shot. My daddy was, after all, a gentle man."

The boy Albert brought out a dinner of roasted quail, candied yams, and canned okra and served out full portions for all three plates and then put the crockery away before sitting down next to the widow.

She was watching Hiram. "I can tell by the looks of you that you take the liquor."

Hiram smiled. "I'm not averse to a slim drink ever now and again, if you're offering."

Her face drew tight. "You do have presumption, I'll give you that."

Despite her rebuke, she brought down a jar of peach brandy from the sideboard and tumped out a small jigger apiece. "For finding cause to stop, Mr. Tobit."

"Yes, ma'am." He returned her toast and together they drank.

Once he had sat for a proper time with Mrs. Stark, listening to her gentle reprimands and repudiations directed against the generally sad state of mankind—and there was no shortage of this, as she attested as a lifelong inhabitant of Canon City who had witnessed every of species of evil in

Sanction County—Hiram excused himself for the evening and went up to his room. He climbed into the long, narrow bed so soft and deep and was almost lost from this world before the old fears laid siege to him. He tossed in the bed and cursed the palest burn of moonlight at the window as cause for his wakefulness, but he knew it was the familiar enemies he was fighting, and they were not going to flee this long night without inflicting some wound. When he could no longer bear the darkness, he crossed the room in bare feet and lit one of two candles set out on the battered armoire. The candle flame revealed only a shallow depth in his surroundings.

Old ghosts kept to these mountains. In running from them, Hiram had thought he put them away, dispelled them somehow. But he now saw himself for the fool he was. Coming back into the hill country, he realized he was the one who haunted the land. Those ghosts, they belonged here more than he ever would. His mother belonged. Kite belonged. But he never truly had. Never would.

His dead brother reached out for him across the years. How many? Nearly ten now. Nearly a decade since Hiram's father had stumbled out drunk, looking to kill coyotes at the chickens and instead pulled the trigger at some movement in the twilit laurel. Just twelve years old and bled on a fool's altar. Buried out there with a secrecy that was worthless because every man, woman, and child in the county had heard the story. And that was why he would always hate his father—for the humiliation, for the reminder that his name would always be part of their family shame.

He eased his weight into the rocker and turned his face to the night outside his window, readying himself for another sad stretch of hours without rest.

Three

It was always the picture of the dress uniform that drew them. The sky-blue trousers, creased like pieces of a perfect body joined and mended, the cobalt tunic with piping the color of autumn leaves aflame. A length of soft armor that could be tailor fit.

Hiram had made the recruiting office as serviceable as possible, tacking up posters and erecting a pair of flags, one for country and one for Corps. He had also framed several photographs of platoons he'd graduated as a drill instructor in his year at Parris Island. Their vacant boy faces stared out from the black and white pictures like rows of tin soldiers, automatic and hateful.

The only problem—and it really had become a serious distraction—was the racket next door. That office was leased by a man by the name of Silvers, prized all throughout the region for his lavish coffins. He was ever slamming and sawing at beams and boards, intent on sending off the wealthy dead in high style. It could certainly grate on a man's nerves. Hiram planned to nail up a panel of cork to keep out the sound, but simply hadn't found time yet.

He sent the first pair of volunteers off within a month, a couple of cousins just turned nineteen. Tall boys with dark country skin and a tendency to lope. He went down with them on the shallow draught barge as far as the mica mine where they could catch the satellite spur of the railway. He shook their hands and looked them in the eye when he promised them they would soon be introduced to a whole new world. Once they boarded and the train carried them off toward the Carolina lowlands, he stood there on the platform long enough to watch the great green barrier of the forest collapse on their departure. Part of him regretted seeing the boys go. But at least he knew there was no war waiting at the far end of the tracks. He took the gray horse the five miles back to town and sat unbothered in his office for the rest of the day.

It was nearly a week before someone else visited.

A pale fist tapped the inside of the doorframe, rousing Hiram from a dozing spell. He blinked and welcomed Reverend Hopper in and invited him to sit. The little man turned in circles as he looked down at the chair lightly dusted with sawdust stirred from the woodworking next door. He finally went to roost only after he had veiled a thin white handkerchief across the seat.

"I'm afraid we're gonna have to do some fancy numbers on you if you aim to sign up, Reverend. We tend to like 'em a little younger."

The silver tipped man looked across the desk at Hiram in a minor state of bafflement until he realized the tone had been joking. A short laugh caught in his throat and he patted a stray lick of white hair behind his ear. "No, no, no. I was hoping to extend an invitation."

"An invitation?"

"Yes, to join our congregation this Sabbath."

Hiram opened the drawer of his desk and rifled through a stack of papers for his pack of cigarettes. He placed his last Camel between his lips and struck a match. "I don't see as how I'm worthy of a personal visit, but I'd be happy to come along and say hello."

"Excellent, we will be looking for you then." Reverend Hopper remained perched on his seat.

"Is there something else I can do for you?"

"Well, there is a point of concern. A minor matter really."

Hiram waited.

"Many members of the congregation have expressed a desire that you not allow these boys to sign contracts for service in the army..."

"The Marine Corps."

"Yes, I'm sorry. The Marines...without first discussing the matter with the parents."

Hiram breathed out and let the preacher wince in the dusty sulk of the office made claustrophobic by the cigarette smoke. "I hope the congregation don't feel I'm taking advantage of their young'uns. That would be a shame."

"Oh, I don't think it is as much that, as a desire to feel a part of their children's decision. We mountain people can be rather clannish."

Hiram smiled to himself. He knew Hopper had as much mountain in him as the Kaiser. "Well, Reverend, these boys are all grown up. They can do what they want with their lives."

The queer little man's features withered.

"But I don't see the harm in invitin' in the parents if they want to hear what I have to say. It's the boys that come to me anyway. I just answer their questions. You and me are alike in that regard, I imagine."

The reverend blinked myopically. "I'm afraid I don't understand, Sergeant."

"Well, you can't make men follow the laws of God if they don't want to. You just let them know you'll be around talking about the good book and how to live in step with the Almighty if they so choose. Can't make them do right, just let them know the difference between right and wrong and then have them pick a side. Same as what I do. A man can live like a man or live for himself. Whatever he chooses is what marks him for the rest of his life. I just make sure he knows there's a choice. A place beyond these mountains."

"Ah, yes. I see." Hopper gained his feet and tucked his handkerchief inside his jacket pocket. "Well, Sgt. Tobit, I must be off. I have to see about some wives who have promised a treat of baked goods after the service this Sunday."

"Sure, wives can be demanding on a man's time, I've heard."

Hopper pressed his lips into a smile, dropped his head and was out of the office without another word.

Once the reverend had cleared the building, Hiram crossed the room to the window and watched him stride to the other side of the square. He wondered at the fact he had attracted the attention of the Lord Almighty's representative in such a short period of time. While he'd expected some outcry among the townsfolk, he was amazed that the first two boys he sent off should gain him a reputation. He tried not to resent Hopper for his interference. The piddly little man was simply carrying out the wishes of his public, but there was something in his puniness that irked. It put Hiram out of his mood beyond all reason and he knew he would be unable to abide the confines of the office for the rest of the day. He snatched his campaign hat off its nail in the wall, flipped the sign in the window to closed and paced back to the Stark boarder house.

He went straight around to the stall where the gray horse was put up with his only companion, Albert's half-blind mule, a creature so accustomed to its uniformly dim surroundings as to not suffer the slightest pang of distress in its habitual state of neglect. Hiram did not even bother to speak to it as he saddled the horse. The mule, for its part, betrayed no signs of disfavor.

He rode to the river, working toward a worn trail scuffed down to powder, watching the runs and riffles of the water pouring out of the wilderness beyond, all of the pent energy of the short but intense winter released in a measured calamity of motion and sound neither terrible nor complete. The earth had made its first turn toward the fertile time of year, mending fresh grass and sylvan boughs. But the air remained cold and the sky just seemed to itch.

After he passed beyond sight of the town, he decided to go in the river for a dip. He stripped out of his uniform and folded and nestled it safely among some doghobble weeds. Once he'd eased into the water to his waist, he ducked his head beneath the surface and bucked back up. The cold drilled into his pores, firing his nerves like hot candle wax.

He swam out to the middle of a deep pool and let himself drift in the circling current. A brook trout broke the surface just at the rim of a stony ledge, darted beneath the marble calm and ripped the water once more, torquing itself into a high, muscular arc. He drifted towards where the fish had disappeared and stood on the mica-flecked bottom looking for any signs of what drew the trout's antics, but saw only the shadowy flitting shapes of minnows flushed from their cubbies.

When he slogged back to the sandy bank to retrieve his uniform he was so struck by the chill of the fresh air that he did not think to take account of the horse's whereabouts. He crouched amid the tall weeds and patted himself dry with the back of his tunic and hastily drew on his small clothes and trousers. He felt strong and revitalized by his quick plunge. He resolved to make a regular habit of it. When he stood, he spied the horse up near the next bend of the river. He set his hat on his head, tossed the tunic over his shoulder, and kept to the easy riverside path, closing quickly on the horse's ambling pace.

Once he was within a hundred yards, he realized the animal wasn't alone. It was hard to see for the leaning chickweed and parsnip, but someone was beside the gray, moving alongside it at the same unhurried speed. Hiram's first impulse was to shout out, but he thought better of giving away his position. Whoever was out there would have time to flee before he could cover the distance. He stayed concealed behind the bristling cover of the riverbank weeds and circled up along the wooded hillside.

After cautiously making his circuit, he came around a big deadfall poplar tree and waited for the horse and the stranger to pass. But they were slow in coming. They paused and wandered in and out of little coves and arbors. It soon became evident that whoever was down there had no intention of theft. Hiram broke from his hiding place to see what stripe of mischief had discovered him.

It was a little girl, perhaps nine or ten, dressed in a dark red flannel dress so long it was a wonder she didn't trip when she walked. She wore a man's black slouch hat, the flopped brim hanging down low so that she couldn't have seen more than a few feet in front of her. The horse shuffled behind, occasionally pausing to crop bracken.

"You ain't the scariest horse thief I met."

She glanced up at him, betraying not the slightest tickle of concern. "You ain't the best horse keeper I've seen, neither. Besides, I didn't aim to take him. He just started following me."

"I didn't know he was bad to do that."

"Well, maybe you the one making him bad."

Hiram took the gray horse by the bridle and walked it up to where the little girl was turning around with her eyes latched to the forest floor. "What you aiming to find?"

"My baby."

He pulled the tunic over his skivvy shirt and righted his hat. "I wouldn't have taken you as having a baby. You ain't a witch woman in disguise as a young'un, by chance?"

She shook her head in exasperation but did not favor him with the briefest glance. "It ain't a real baby, Mister Soldier Man. I'm talking about my old raggedy doll. Some boys done took it."

"Took it?"

"Yeah, took it. Stoled it."

They walked on through the woods for a quiet piece, searching the ground for some evidence of the missing playpretty.

"Why'd they steal it?"

"'Cause they mean little boys and that's what mean little boys do, as far as I can tell."

"I guess there's no arguing that. What does she look like?"

She stopped and drove the palms of her hands against her bony hips. "Well, to start, it weren't a she. It were a little boy with red yarny hair. He was sporting a pair of dungarees and a gingham shirt. So if you see anything like that, give a holler." She tramped off along an abandoned game trail too narrow for Hiram to bring the horse, turning her pink face over her shoulder. "You take the river walk. I'll check up here among some of the hidey holes I know about."

Thus formally deputized into the manhunt, Hiram moved off through a sun-striped clearing, tugging at the horse to come along against that creature's natural choice of following the girl. It wasn't long before he found the victim with a nail driven between his eyes against a fir tree. Hiram tried to get his fingers between the canvas and the bark to draw the doll out neat, but the boys had been zealous in their execution.

"You'd better take a look at this."

The little girl came crashing down the hill kicking leaves, but pulled up short when she saw what he'd found. "I knew it'd be something like that. Can't get the nail out, can you?"

He shook his head.

She walked past and pointed herself up on teetering toes to get a closer look. Without hesitation, she grabbed hold of the doll's chubby ears and ripped it down, the sawdust inside tumbling out. Hiram considered saying some words of comfort, but before he could, the little girl was already back on the path the way she came, the doll's limp body swinging under her arm. He followed her back out as far as the bridge before he gained the saddle with a creak of leather and rode past, tipping his hat and wishing her the best of the afternoon.

She gave a short wave. "I imagine my afternoon ain't much more than stitching by the looks of old Isaac here."

"You want a ride then?"

"Naw, I ain't got far to go. Thank you, Soldier Man." She dipped into a quick curtsy before charging up the riverbank and dropping out of sight, the empty space of her going a fixed spot on the earth.

Four

When Sunday arrived Hiram found he wasn't the only member of the household bound across the river for church. Albert was released from his chores long enough to take the necessary bread of spiritual enlightenment, though his mother warned not to tarry afterwards or risk the punishment of cleaning out the chicken house. Hiram was surprised to find the widow herself would not be in attendance given her averred piety, but didn't mention a word of this as he was happy to have the boy alone as his companion on the walk across. They left early to clear out before the widow remembered some chore that needed Albert's attention. Leaving at such an hour had them sitting outside the church cemetery, waiting for the rest of the congregation to show up.

In the time they had, Hiram pointed out the different birds darting through the morning trees and gave Albert their proper names. He was surprised how little of the natural world the boy knew. Too long in the widow's service with pots and pans and not enough in the woods, Hiram believed. Fathers were good for that, at least.

"How'd did your daddy pass, Albert?"

The boy pressed a half moon into the ground with the heel of his boot. "He were away on a business trip when it happened. Selling tack over in Asheville. Momma said his heart blew up on him from all the drinking."

"You miss him?"

Albert shrugged. "Sometimes I feel like the dead ain't dead. I still see him sometimes at night. He's standing over in the corner of the room by the window covered up with all those nighttime shadows. He don't ever say nothing and he don't ever make a move, but I can see how his eyes watch me. Do you believe in haints?"

"I guess a man would be a fool to disbelieve something he don't know anything about."

"Then you ain't never seen one?"

Hiram plucked a stem of tall grass and tamped it in the corner of his mouth.

"Hell, I don't know, maybe. I guess it's hard to tell whether a thing is real or not when it comes to dealing with haints."

Albert nodded his head solemnly. "Now, I guess that does make a heap of sense."

The front doors of the church yawned open and Reverend Hooper popped out like a furious cuckoo, setting his stones at the jambs to block the hinges from swinging shut. Once he'd straightened up and surveyed the still empty front lot, he cast his gaze over toward the cemetery and saw Hiram and Albert. "Good morning, Sgt. Tobit! I see you are recruiting new members to the house of the Lord as well. Perhaps our roles are as similar as you suggest after all." The preacher did not wait for a response, drawing back inside the church for whatever practice demanded his attention there.

Albert looked at where the little man had disappeared. "He's a strange little feller, ain't he?"

"I won't argue it. Come on and let's get us a seat before all the choice spots are picked."

The empty pews stretched the length of each side of the puncheon-floored aisle, ranked before the little stage with its pulpit and the carved crèche scene affixed to the back wall. Hiram and Albert slid in at a corner beneath a window of stained glass, the golden dial of the savior's halo spread warmly across them in the morning sun. Within a few minutes, the congregation began its hushed entry. Most carried their own Bibles, black-leathered tomes as heavy as gunmetal. Their shoes clopped roughly over the bare floor as they edged their way past one another, saying their quiet apologies and hellos as they waited for the reverend to appear.

The little man came out in the plain dress of his everyday ministry and spoke his greetings. The people of the church answered and all bent their necks before the wooden image of the infant Christ and let the official words of benediction pass over them.

The words were so familiar to Hiram. The same his mother had spoken throughout his boyhood. The easy praise and the submission to his will. How those words worked at him now, though. All the faith and humility armies of men could summon up meant nothing when the heart of God turned hard. Hiram had listened to the screams of the dying in his name, whether it was in English or German. But his answer never varied, all human language apparently beyond his ken. Hiram turned his eyes up before the final Amen. He saw that others did too.

Once Hopper preached to the noon hour, they all said their departing prayer and adjourned to the shaded backyard where the good wives had spread their baked goods on long tables. At the end of the serving board sat several coffee pots still blackened from sitting on the fire. Hiram and the boy each gathered a slice of warm buttered cornbread and a mug of black coffee and leaned against a cottonwood tree by the river, watching the other members of the church walk through the languid peace of the Sunday afternoon still coming.

"You ain't gonna get your momma mad at me for having you to stay around a while, I hope?"

Albert chewed a little shape out of his cornbread and dusted away a shower of crumbs that fell to the lapel of his jacket. "She ain't gonna be mad at nobody but me. I figure I can take it."

Hiram followed Albert's gaze to a pretty little blond girl sitting by the riverbank with her father and mother. She had a green bow the size of an oak leaf in her long soft hair. "I guess you could tell me all about her, couldn't you?"

Albert hooked his finger in his collar to draw a space for breathing. "She's just a girl, is all."

"You know her name?"

"Naw. I've just seen her about now and then. I don't know nothing about who her folks is."

"You gonna get to know her, then?"

Albert ignored Hiram and his joking and went back to his cornbread.

"Sgt. Tobit, you should introduce me to your young friend here." This from Reverend Hopper, appearing from a small knot of chattering townsmen who made a distant study of Hiram and the boy.

Albert put out his hand and introduced himself to the preacher and retreated into a faint silence. Hiram sipped his coffee and stepped forward. "Looks like you have all the world's aldermen with you, Reverend."

Hopper glanced over his shoulder at the men approaching and loosed one of his high-pitched barks that passed for a laugh. "Yes, these are some members of the congregation who have asked to meet you, Sergeant. First, if I can present you to Judge Spenser."

A narrow-shouldered man wearing a dark suit reached out his thin hand like a pair of calipers and gently tapped the skin of Hiram's palm before drawing back as suddenly as if he had been electrically shocked. "A pleasure to have one of our own heroes come back home. I'm right in that you are a mountain native?"

"Yes, sir, your Honor. I grew up a piece away from Canon City."

"Ah, very good." The judge's mint green eyes briefly abstracted. Quickly recovering, he cleared his throat. "This is my son Gerald, a veteran like yourself..."

The judge's son nodded beneath a straw hat with a red silk band. Unlike his father, he was tall, dark, and happy to remain socially disengaged. Hiram placed his manner somewhere between snobbish and indifferent.

"And this bear of a fellow is Sheriff Alex Painter."

The sheriff put out his great soft hand and nearly wrapped his index finger around to his thumb when he gripped Hiram's palm in a handshake. "A great thing to have another dependable man in our town, Sergeant. It makes this old lawman feel a bit better knowing a reliable man is just down the way from the courthouse." The sheriff tugged his enormous silver mustache into an unctuous smile.

Despite these few pleasantries, Hiram immediately knew he was being gauged by these men.

"Shouldn't you mention the deputizing, Alex?" Judge Spenser spoke off to the side, though he made no effort to avoid being overheard.

The sheriff put on an unconvincing show of reluctance before finally coming around to the point. "Well, actually Sgt. Tobit, I'm sure you can appreciate the irony of this. We were actually hoping to recruit you into *our* service." He punctuated his intent with a little glimmer of mischief in his eyes. The sheriff glanced at Reverend Hopper before he continued. "I'm sure there's something blasphemous about taking the Sabbath as an opportunity for enlistment, but I think considering the good motive behind it, the Lord will grant me pardon."

The sheriff informed Hiram of the company of part-time deputies he maintained in times of community crisis. Hiram knew he was not being given a choice whether or not to join this corps but being informed of what was expected of him as a man of public reputation. He finished his coffee, slung out the dregs and said he would be pleased to sign up. *Even here the world makes its small demands of its bloodied sons.* All of the men fixed iron smiles to their faces and said their good days, not wanting to spoil his enjoyment of the picnic, they claimed.

Once they had gone, Hiram and Albert wandered down the river a bit while the rest of the congregation likewise spread from the immediate place of their gathering. The girls played in the sunshine and the boys followed in their wake with their hands in their pockets, stomping earthworms and telling jokes. Their parents linked hands and merely ambled, sometimes watching the frolics and sometimes calling over the heads of their sons and daughters, cautioning them to be careful or nice to one another while they all moved on past the opalescent ring of the sun growing large on the moving water.

"Mister Soldier Man!"

It was the little girl with the doll from a few days before. She was decked in a white church gown already stained from playing on the grass. She skipped around Hiram once in a circle and then touched two fingers to her forehead in salute. He returned the gesture and told her to stand easy.

"How's your baby getting along?"

"Oh, I cinched him up good. Just a little scar where the nail were."

"I'm proud to hear he'll recover."

She squinted at the boy Albert. "He ain't a mean little boy, is he?"

"He's no kidnapper if that's what you're worried about."

"Good, I won't need to worry about this then." She drew a small jackknife from a hidden pocket in her skirt.

"You got protection now, I see."

"You betcha, Soldier Man. I'm ready to kill the next little boy that tries to do away with old Isaac." He sensed by the tone of her voice that she was capable of just that.

From a distance a woman's voice called out. "Note, come on honey, we've got to head back to your granddaddy's."

Hiram turned his head toward the bridge where he saw a dark-haired woman waving a red carpet bag above her head to gain the little girl's attention.

"Note?"

"Look, Soldier Man, I didn't have nothing to do with

my own naming. Why don't you come along and tell my momma how funny you think it is?"

She trudged away before he could give an answer. Hiram told Albert to head on home and went off to meet the young mother waiting by the bridge trestle.

When Hiram came up he saw that Note and her mother had already found themselves at odds. The little girl winced as the woman wiped at the long streaks of dirt at the corner of her ears and down the length of her long browned neck. "How do you stay so filthy, gal? I swear you've grown part dirt dauber."

Note twisted and cried out, winning her freedom only when she brought her mother's attention to the fact that someone had come to meet her.

The woman's beauty wasn't striking, but it was her own. Unlike so many others who had dressed up for the spectacle of church Sunday, Note's mother wore a faded gray dress cut to a simple design, tied up at the waist with a swatch of burgundy that gave dimension to her shape beneath. Her figure was thin but strong, heavy in the breasts and hips. Her features were classical with a pronounced chin and high-planed cheekbones. The large pupils in her soft hazel eyes shone with the luster of obsidian.

Note managed the introductions by way of explaining Hiram as the rescuer of poor old Isaac. He reached his hand out to the woman and spoke his name.

"Cass Chisholm, Mr. Tobit. I guess I have to claim responsibility for this little wild thing." She pinched a length of Note's braid between her fingers like they were a pair of shears.

"I can tell you one thing, Sergeant, I ain't never seen a little gal happier than when she brought back that doll of hers. Sometimes I wonder if she ain't had him since she was in my belly."

Hiram felt his lungs tighten when he tried to find something to say. "I guess she's been having a hard time with some boys whereabout you and your husband live…"

"Ain't no husband, Sergeant."

Hiram's chest just opened. It was as easy and hard as that.

"Momma, have Sergeant come up to supper sometime so he can see how I've done patched up Isaac. I'm sure he'll think a heap of my stitching. Maybe good enough for an army nurse even."

Cass smiled and drew Note against her waist. "We'll have to see if the Sergeant has any other obligations. And that's assuming he favors our company."

A chain of knots slipped inside him. "I would be happy to give my professional opinion, Miss Note. Whenever your momma has time to receive an old rough-mannered man like me."

"Tonight, Momma!"

"We have to visit your granddaddy's tonight, gal."

"Tomorrow then. And he can bring his horse."

"I imagine that's up to him, Note."

The little girl trained pleading eyes. She didn't even have to say a word to draw his assent. He promised to ride up within the next few days. As he walked back to the boarding house, Hiram sensed a mildness in the afternoon, a sweet hint of good walking weather. He breathed it in, filling himself with something like sunlight.

Five

A few weeks later Hiram was taking his regular post-supper brandy with the widow Stark, half listening to her go on about the need for caution as he courted this woman Cass Chisholm. It was a conversation he had grown accustomed to since he'd first begun seeing Note's mother. "She used to be as wild as the young'un of hers 'fore she settled down and married."

He had gradually learned to tolerate the widow's eventide counsel when it concerned his lovemaking. Perhaps his restraint had something to do with the gentling effects drink had on the old woman's otherwise irascible mood. She had just topped them both off from the cut glass decanter when they heard a sharp knock at the front door. Hiram offered to see what interruption had come to pay a visit, but the widow dismissed his courtesy and went to see about the trouble herself.

Sheriff Painter marched in, swung his hat off his head and collapsed in one of the parlor's ladder-back chairs in such a creak and cry of protesting cane it was a wonder it didn't splinter. He huffed and coughed and his enormous hands were already worrying at his pocket watch before he had time to explain why he had come. "Need you and your horse, Sergeant. All hell's broke loose."

Hiram waited for him to catch his breath so he could go on.

"Old Man Vaughn. His youngest went and got herself in trouble with some boy. Seems he got tipped to the fact she's carrying a bastard and like to have a fit. Said if she didn't tell him who the daddy was, he was gonna cut the little rabbit right out of her belly. He's gone and run off and took the girl with him according to the momma. Lit out with the girl last night cussing about how he was gonna show that damn child the price for lying about while she was under his roof. We've got a fair idea of where he's heading and I need ever man who can ride and shoot so as to get that gal back before he proves himself a fool."

Without waiting to hear more, Hiram wrote a brief note to Cass to explain he would be away for perhaps several days and passed it to the widow, making her promise to give it to her should she ask about his absence. The old woman reluctantly consented, begging off that she would take no part in such affairs if it wasn't for the general good of the township. As soon as he'd drawn her assent, he went up and fetched what equipage he needed from his room and met the sheriff at the stable. Once the horse was tacked, they turned on to the main road, slowing down when he passed the front of the boarding house where Mrs. Stark stood with a shawl about her shoulders, watching him go. Because he didn't want her to worry, he lifted his hat to her. She merely shook her head and walked back into her empty parlor.

At the courthouse, they met the rest of the posse, three

boys sitting weak-legged nags in the twilight. With them was the judge's son, Gerald Spenser. His horse was a red Tennessee Walker a good twenty hands high. He held the reins in tailored leather gloves. He leaned from his saddle and spat. "Thought you said you were bringing a passel."

The sheriff glared at Spenser. "He was the only one who answered the door. You boys wait here while I see to our arsenal." The big man lumbered off his horse and went up the stone steps of the courthouse, the heavy oak door swatting shut behind him.

The three boys nodded their hellos to Hiram and introduced themselves as the Price brothers: Johnson, Macon, and Trent. They were big hollow-faced youths with ginger hair sprung like fence wire about their bare heads. The oldest of them couldn't have been more than sixteen.

"Why ain't your daddy out here boys?"

The one name Trent answered Hiram. "He's down in Fayetteville. Gone as a factor with the big mica freight last week. He'd be here if he could. Daddy's powerful eager to get after bad men."

In five minutes the sheriff came out with their rifles and ammunition and handed them up. The firearms were old lever actions with iron butt plates and deeply scarred stocks, mainly good for knocking through heavy brush and not much else. They fed the brass into the tube magazines and either slung the guns across their backs or devised some method of easy stowage outside the saddle straps.

By the time they cleared the edge of town it had grown full dark and seemed blacker yet because the moon had still not risen. The sounds of the horses and the dim trace of shadow against the forest was all they had to keep themselves in single file along the march. The sheriff whistled a tune to orient them as they rode the long climb into the high country. Occasionally he called back words of caution when they were coming through rocky ground liable to snag the hooves of the horses.

It was on past midnight when they crested the top ridgeline and had the great sweep of the whole mountain range dropping off on each side of them with the distant smear of the moon riding low across the southeastern sky. At night the country below looked so much closer than it actually was. Almost enough to trick a man into believing he could step from his horse and cross the whole vista spread out there without breaking a sweat.

They put in at the edge of a bald not long after that, hobbling their horses and snubbing down under their blankets to get what rest they could before continuing the pursuit at first light. Hiram was asleep without even realizing he'd left the world of the waking.

That night he dreamed of being born on a cold dark planet under a sky of moonlight so weak it did not even cast a glint among the acres of gunmetal planted row upon row. He knew the silent flashes over the horizon were the big guns opening up on some distant plain. The men beside him in the trenches slept untroubled under their coats and ponchos. He wondered at their unconsciousness, gripping his Springfield rifle so tightly it could have been a splint for his fist. Then he was out of the trenches, alone, carried to No Man's Land on a dream wind. A German sentry spotted him and cried out, and a volley of rifle fire plowed the ground at his feet. He sprinted for the cover of a crater.

He was on his stomach. The hammering of Maxim machine guns pounded the dirt, turning clots of mud. He looked back to see if any of the men in his trench had followed, but there were no signs of them and he knew they were still asleep in the safety of their dugouts. Flares washed over him in drifting angles of light. Shadows on the crater's wall grew huge and grotesque, the nodding antennae of insects as long as a man's arm. He closed his eyes. The crater began to collapse and the running grains of soil flowed from the crumbling rim like the roiling of snakes. He climbed for the surface but the ground gave way at every step.

Somehow he made his way out. He ran forward once more, dashing for the German lines until he met the obstruction of bodies. They were built into a parapet, stacked and mortared with their own gore. Their eyes had been bayoneted so that their pursed sockets dribbled cloudy tears of pus. Their bodies gave muscular jerks as the incoming fire plucked their ligaments like piano wires.

He felt a hand on his shoulder. Without looking, he recognized the touch of his mother. She sat down beside him and sang one of the hymns of his childhood. The machine gunfire grew more sporadic until it ceased completely. He could hear a faint baritone echo of her singing repeated in the enemy's trenches. When it grew silent, she rose and led him around the wall of dead soldiers. Her long church dress swept the ground so that he couldn't see her feet or hear the sound of her steps. Another cry went up and the rifle and machine gunfire renewed. He ran for the German lines, but his mother blocked him. She was struck by the rain of iron, but still she advanced as the bullets stripped away her flesh. She walked on, hacked down to nothing but her bones and heart.

The next morning was warm and they did not bother with

cooking fires before they fed the horses. Their own brief meal was whatever private stores they had managed to tuck away in their saddlebags along with a cup of creek water. Sheriff Painter promised they would find a place to stop by midday so that they could have a chance to properly fill their bellies.

Early on there was no inclination to talk, but as the day grew hot and the Price boys became more curious about what they should expect, they discussed the possibilities among themselves before the oldest brother, Johnson, rode up to the sheriff and asked where they were headed and what he intended to have them do.

The sheriff removed a masticated cigar from his lips. "When we get there you'll know it. When I have you do something, you'll do it."

The boys looked at each other and then resumed their place in the march.

The sheriff made good on his promise for a hot meal when they came into Lincoln, having their horses watered while they went into the hotel for plates of fried chicken and biscuits as big as a man's palm. He had the Price boys eat first so they could go look to the horses while he, Hiram, and Spenser had a chance to talk alone.

"Mrs. Vaughn said her husband is likely holed up at the old abandoned deer camp about ten miles north, up in the upper end of Sanction County. I understand you know that area pretty good, Sergeant?"

Hiram nodded. "Know it fair. Daddy took me up there a few times. Not much more than a couple of fire pits and a clearing as I can remember."

"Well, apparently they've strung together a few shanties since then. Nobody hunts up there anymore, but it's known as a place for gambling and drinking. It's so far out of the way of everything these days. I was hoping you could take the lead in tracing the way there."

"I guess I can manage that."

Once the order of the day was fully settled, they cleared their plates, tramped off the hip-roofed porch where they'd eaten for the benefit of a breeze, and crossed into the full heat of the afternoon where the horses were already made ready. On the way out of the village they passed the peat house where Atlanta lived and Hiram wondered how well she and Henry might be getting along. He wondered too if the family life was something as easy to possess as Henry made it seem.

Within the hour, the sky grew a mealy yellow where the weak sun dribbled through granite cloudbanks. No birds were flying and the wind had completely died away. The horses labored under the burden of the weather. It became clear they had to find some shade and stop until the languid heat broke. The best the riders could do was hunker down in a maze-like arbor of rhododendron where fleas and mosquitoes were the only creatures alive under the weight of such misery. The men made themselves small in the pencil-etched shadows, swatting at the bugs while they tried to keep their movement to a minimum. A storm was coming.

The weather slammed into the mountains. Treetops bowed under the sharp wind and high branches cracked and toppled through the vast canopy, landing on the earth with muffled thuds. The thunder quaked the ground and the hail beat down on their shelter like teeth scattered. The horses stepped and sidled and the men tried to keep them as calm as they could.

Once the hail passed, the rain grew harder and colder

and the channeled ground beneath the rhododendron began to flood. The men had to shout to be heard above the din. They evacuated hastily and lost many of their loose supplies. The youngest Price boy somehow managed to leave his rifle behind and the sheriff drove him back into the thicket with vulgar oaths and sat with the rain plastering his hat to his skull until the boy came back out with the muddy firearm slung across his back.

Hiram led them up to the abandoned causeway, hoping to get clear of the floodplain, but when they met the hoofbeaten trail, they found it leached weak from the pouring watershed. The horses were bad to slip and it was a miracle they got back off the trace within a mile without breaking any of their legs. They rode down to a stone outcropping and sat figuring while the rain slapped the gutted bluffs enveloping them.

"This ain't stopping anytime soon." Hiram waved his hat dry, knowing it would be soaked again as soon as they rejoined the trail.

The sheriff squatted, joints snapping. "No, I figure it won't. You think we should settle down here?"

Hiram shook his head. "Shoot, those boys would desert from the plain empty-belliedness of it."

They looked over at the Price boys who were drawn up in a small circle with one another, a gathering of clammy skins and suffering. Not a single one had spoken a word since the storm set in.

"Well, we did lose what vittles we had back there in the laurel. I guess we could turn back to Lincoln. Stay there until this weather lets."

Hiram spat. "No way we could make it back before dark.

We've got to go somewhere closer that won't take us too far off the old man's track."

"What you figuring, then?"

Hiram watched the long, dark fog running the length of the valley and the rain daggering the earth. "Have 'em saddle up. We'll ride on to my daddy's place. I can't think of a reason not to."

The second taste of cold and wet was a hard thing to bear. While the riders had merely shivered before, now it was as though their bones were trying to shake clear out of their joints. The Price boys made the mistake of piling on every piece of clothing they could, leaving them drenched and needlessly weighted. For all their swaddling, they bore the discomfort of the elements with a furious pride and sullenness even though the older men tried to tell them better. They coughed and complained and Hiram knew if he didn't get those boys to a clean, dry place before nightfall, they were liable to go off and do something reckless.

When they came up to Black's Creek it was well out of its regular banks. The water screamed and ran a full frothing white. Storm-wrecked tree limbs wheeled past with great resounding cracks as they struck obstructions hidden beneath the dam slides. Spenser tried to breast the crossing with his big Tennessee Walker, but the current was too strong, and before he could venture a quarter of the way across, he was nearly thrown to the fates. He came tottering back up the crumbling bank, horse and man alike streaming and agasp. Once the others could see that he was all right and able to continue, they turned their horses upstream and rode with the impassable creek just a few yards away.

Six

In the complete dark Hiram sat watching where he thought the bridge must lie. He heard the other horses ranged up behind him, stepping and shying. He checked the knotted rope looped through his saddle's rigging dee and tugged it once to make sure it was running straight back to the next horse in the line. He turned his head over his shoulder and saw Trent Price raise his hand. Beyond the boy's shape Hiram could see nothing. He would have to trust the rope to keep the others aligned with him. He swung back around in the saddle and had his horse ease up a couple of steps and they all shuffled a few feet closer to the roaring stream.

The rain continued. It had been falling for a good eight hours now and even what ground wasn't flooded had grown soft and spongy. Ongoing fits of wind beat and deformed the trees. Hiram couldn't be certain his landmarks were true. The storm had cleaved the ground, choking the earth with turned stones and roots that hadn't clutched. The gray horse tossed its head at the water and balked and began to back away. Hiram drove his knees down hard and spoke to it in a whisper and once more it answered his command, stepping off blindly into the creek.

The animal's forelegs sunk as deep as the cannon bone before the hooves struck the hidden planking below. The surge of water nearly ripped Hiram's boots free. He leaned down with his head just above the crest of the gray's neck and sang a soft tune to quiet it as they traversed the flooded bridge.

The rest of the party shuffled behind. The rope snapped taut as the working horseflesh strained to keep interval against the charging current. Halfway across one of the horses reared invisibly in the dark and Hiram could feel the gray horse lean back under the burden, the slanted rush of the waters and the tension of the rope wrenching away. The men's yells and oaths were swallowed by the wailing of the beast. Hiram drove his heels hard and clawed his fingers into the mane, and the gray answered and pulled until they lunged clear, great gouts of floodwater sluicing onto solid ground from both man and horse. The others scrambled in, all of them breathing great gasps, a gathering of survivors terrible, amphibious, and humbled.

Once they had completely gained the opposite bank, they worked the joining rope free and Spenser coiled it over his shoulder as they rode up to Sloane's cabin. The old man had heard them coming and stood blocking the yellow rectangle of the open doorway, a long shotgun trailing from his arm like poorly set bone.

Hiram got off his horse and went up to where the rain scattershot across the tin roof.

Sloane's voice bit like a hatchet. "I guess I was expecting you."

"How's that?"

"I just knew, is all." The old man turned his eyes out to the streaming dark beyond. "Who are they?"

"The law. Looking for a man that made a mess of things."

Sloane nodded and spat over the far edge of the porch floorboards. "They's plenty of that type around, I imagine."

"You gonna put us up until this storm passes?"

He leaned the shotgun against the doorframe. "I guess I'd be a sumbitch not to. How you set up all them horses is your business. Once you got that figured, bring those boys on in for a smoke and a cup."

Hiram turned to the horses.

"Hiram."

"Yes, sir?"

"It's been a long time coming home."

The riders rigged what scraps of canvas they carried from the edge of the porch roof and strung it down with guy ropes so that the horses were nudged up together under a dripping lean-to. The Price boys went around and made each horse fast to the railing and left them to suffer the night as best they could while the riders shook the rain off before entering the cabin.

Sloane had made good on his promise, laying out a full setting of mugs encircling a pitcher of moonshine. Each of the riders said words of thanks and filled the drinking vessels to the brim before they found some place to station themselves in the dim front room. The old man offered them tobacco as well, though he only had three pipes. They all declined so as not to put one another to disadvantage. Once they turned to drinking, Sloane asked what had drawn them out on this forsaken night. The sheriff detailed the kidnapping escapade of the man named Vaughn. Sloane listened to the whole story before he closed his eyes against the glimmer of the lantern light and nodded.

"Matthew Vaughn?"

Sheriff Painter looked up. "Yes, sir. That's the feller. How do you know him?"

"Hunted with him a few times over the years. I'm guessing he's run off for the old deer camp?"

Sheriff Painter looked round at his men. "That's what we're figuring. Seems a likely place for a man to run once he's backed up against a wall."

Sloane rested his head against his chair's backrest and stared up at the ceiling, seeming to hold some unspoken point of interest in his mind. "Old Matt ain't a dangerous man unless he's made to be. I hope you and my son take that into account when you ride up there after him."

The sheriff worked his broad face into a genial smile. "Why sure, Mr. Tobit. We're just up to make sure he doesn't hurt himself or anybody else. Seeing as how you know the feller yourself, maybe you would consider coming along when the storm passes. It would be a great service to all involved if you were to give Mr. Vaughn a familiar face to turn to."

Hiram stepped forward. "I don't see as how he could manage to keep up with that hobble of his. Besides, he ain't got nothing to ride, other than that broke-legged mule."

Sloane watched Hiram.

Johnson Price stood unsteadily, his young face inflamed from drink. "You would be welcomed to doubling up with one of us, Mr. Tobit."

"Mighty kind, young man. Mighty kind indeed. I'll have to chew on it for a bit. There ain't any decisions need to be made this evening anyhow from the sounds of that rain, am I right, Sheriff?"

Painter agreed that he was.

The pitcher of moonshine circled freely round. To pass the time stories were exchanged. Old stories that carried the distinct pauses and rhythms of tales crafted over time and perfected through repetition. Some efforts were better than others, but each speaker strove to best the last. Hiram knew it would only be so long before his father told the old family story, the one he had heard so often as a boy and repeated later on down unto the days before he left his mountain home for the war. He stepped back to the kitchen and scuffed out a chair, sitting alone. In the next room he heard his father clear his throat. Sloane was about to tell that old lie. Hiram knew the old man could tell it so well.

This is a true war story what happened to my daddy.

It was either '64 or '65, depending on when he told it to you. Either way, he was about fifteen years old when he run off and stole a mule named Jonas from his own daddy so he could ride on to fight with the rebs. He figgered they'd make a horseman out of him since he brought along his own mule and equipage. He knew they were in a sorry state as it was with Sherman and his army burning up ever'thing in its path and even a lowly mule would be better than what most other boys his age would've brung, which weren't nothing more than an empty belly.

Well, he was right. Though he'd been better suited to fife and drum than mounted soldering, they took him. You see, he was a humble-looking boy. I still have his likeness from the army on an old tintype. Face as broad as a bull's, simple-looking. It had to be so, 'cause we're talking here of men hard on the campaign nigh on four years. They weren't about to let some young son ride into their camp and that's all there was to it. No, sir. He musta reminded them of boys they's left back home, brothers or sons, maybe. So they not only took him, they adopted him into the company. Made a mascot out of him. Gave him charms to protect him from the war. Trinkets such as minié balls what were turned aside by blind luck, a knife blade or pannikin or some such. The iron bullet flat as biscuit dough from where it struck the lucky spot.

Now, he was an Army of Tennessee man through and through. Even up unto the day he died he used to tell me he ain't never seen such a fine group of fellers. He loved the nights around the fire, listening to all those men telling him stories of the battles they'd fought, the things they'd seen. He loved their songs too, some so lonesome and true.

One thing those soldiers loved about him was he could pick a banjer. I mean, he was flat scary with it. When the other soldiers found this out, there weren't no end to the time they'd keep him up late strumming that old thing. Lord knows where it come from. I suppose armies got room for just about ever'thing. Even the colonel would come down from his tent to hear him play like the devil.

When it came to riding, he did a piece of that too, running dispatches between the company commander and the brigade. Even so, he was eager to get him a real bite out of the war. He was afraid it was getting away from him, see, and he didn't want to have got into all that trouble over that stole mule without some reward of it. He went to the captain and said he was willing to do just about anything to get on the next mounted patrol. By and by, he got his wish.

It was a foraging party sent out to see if the Yanks had overlooked any of the homesteads thereabouts. They were at it most of a day, riding up long driveways that looked promising, but most everything had been picked over clean. Big houses left with the doors standing open and emptier than a lawyer's conscience on the inside. Well, they had but one more place to check and their spirits was faring mighty poorly.

The captain, he was so down at heart from all that useless searching, he didn't even ride up to see about that last house on the dirt road. Sent my daddy on ahead to have him report back. Well, there must have been some brand of Providence in him deciding that. But what did my daddy find up at that old house? Cribs full of laid-by corn and more than a dozen deep stacks of canned veggies, greens, okra, what have you. When he rode back to the rest of the party they took him for pulling a prank. Said he was a cruel-hearted little son to pretend such things. But he managed to convince them soon enough and they all rode back to the home place to see what might be had for the taking.

It was a sight more than they could carry themselves, being lightly equipped for the scouting. The captain, he sent daddy back to brigade headquarters. Signed a sheet and said to take it to the colonel so they could send teams and wagons to haul off the booty. The rest of the party stayed there, keeping an eye to the vittles.

Now, this was some bona fide adventuring, Daddy thought as he rode. Two heaping armies crawling around in the Carolina brush after one another and him riding dispatch through the middle of it. His blood, it was slamming in his ears like a fencepost being hammered home. He musta had so much heroic deeds going on inside his head he didn't see the first of the horsemen because he was still riding hell for leather straight on the open causeway when the first shot was fired.

He damn near had to strangle Jonas to pull up short. The

pistol balls was all about him. It was a good thing those Yankees hadn't thought to put a carbine bead on him, cause that would've been the end of the Tobit line right then and there. But that wasn't about to make a difference here in a minute cause here them blue-coated cavalry come whooping and a-hollering up the road, their horses just beating the ground all to hell to get at Daddy and his footsore mule.

Now, Daddy knew those boys' horses were a damn sight faster than poor old Jonas. So he turned straight off the road into some of the ugliest cane and briar you could imagine. All flooded bottomlands with the mud dredged up, smelling like a privy house. He knowed if them cavalrymen thought anything of their horses, there wasn't much chance they'd haul in there after him. And he was right, they weren't about to waste themselves or their animals on chasing some damn fool boy across the devil's back acres. But what he didn't count on is that they wouldn't let him go without giving him another run for his money. And this is when them carbines got unscabbarded. Ever' one of them Yankees took a crack at him, kicking up bullets all through that swamp. One of the shots, it got him too.

He could hear them laughing when he cried out from the pain. The ball hit him in the back just a jot below his shoulder blade and carried clean through out from underneath his armpit. Nasty as could be, a real gusher, but at least the bullet wasn't stuck inside him. I don't reckon he thought to offer up a prayer of thanks at the time, though. He was just plumb miserable with the pain and couldn't get it to stop bleeding.

Once he was sure the riders weren't set on following him, he got down off his mule and went through his saddlebags for some cotton rags and fashioned hisself a bandage. By now it was nighttime and dark as the damned and he was turned around something awful. There wasn't no way he was going to be riding out of that swamp until sunup. He was so worn out and dizzy from all that blood that had poured out on the dirt, he didn't even bother with making some place to sleep. He just found a solid piece of ground and fainted dead away.

When he come to the next morning, the mule was gone. Old Jonas, in the middle of all that wild country, must have decided it was time to see to his own best interests. A fog had rolled in and when my daddy tried to find his way through it, it wasn't any better than it had been when it was pitch dark. Well, it didn't take much walking through this to turn him desperate. You got to remember he was still just a boy at the time, and here he was with more of this war business he'd ever counted on. He spent all morning trying to trace his steps back to the road but the ground was so soft that the water flooded a set of tracks a soon as they were laid. He couldn't make the first bit of sense of where he'd come from or how to get back to the road.

By around noontime the sun had burned enough of the fog off that he could see where the land sloped upwards and turned into a little tongue of hard ground that looked promising. He stumbled on through them woods, having to take a rest ever now and then on account of the wound a throbbing in his shoulder. It had taken on a cold ache and he knew he needed to find some help soon or that limb would be nothing but a bitter memory.

Well, by and by, he did come out of that swamp and into somebody's back property. He could see the old homeplace from the bottom of the hill and he eyeballed it a long time to see if there was anybody stirring. He didn't spy nothing, so he went on up to get a better handle on the situation.

The place was plumb wrecked. The Yankees had put the torch to it and about half had burned before God or man had done something to interfere. It had collapsed in on itself, but there was still plenty of spaces in there that might hide provisions, so he poked his head inside. When he did, he got the whiff of the most God-awful stink you can imagine. He knew right away it was something dead that had been that way a good long time. As rough as he felt, though, he went in anyway. He knew he needed to turn up some description of corn liquor to pour over that wound of his quick. He was already starting to feel the tremors of a fever coming on him.

He rooted 'round amid all the scorched timbers and broke joists, turning over ever' piece of furniture in the place. With the smell, he was near to gagging, but he kept up at it till he found half a glass jar with some likely looking shine. He sniffed it and it sure enough cut through the bad stink of the house at large. He turned it up to his mouth to take the edge off what he knew he needed to do, and then he poured a little trickle over the wound. Once he'd done that, he decided it was a right good idea to go ahead and finish off what whiskey what was still in the jar. Before he knew it, he was out for the night.

He woke the next morning to a double-bore shotgun on his head. He could see it was dawn through the broken roof, but he couldn't see nothing of the face of whoever had the drop on him. He blinked his eyes and started to get up but that fowling piece got pressed up square against his chest until Daddy was pinned flat to the dirt.

"Just cuz you ain't wearing blue don't mean I've got any use for you around here," a voice said.

Now, cause he wasn't expecting it, it took him a minute to catch on to the fact that the voice belonged to a woman. Woman or no, he still was willing to take things easy since she hadn't made no move to put that shotgun of hers away.

"I'm hurt," was all he could say. Maybe it was something about that it was said to a female, him remembering they'd been

the ones that took care of him his whole life, but that he came damn near to crying. Well, this got the shadow's attention. She circled round to let a splinter of light prick his face so she could see if he was lying or not. She still kept that shotgun pointed at him though.

"Why you ain't no more than a sprout," she said. "What's wrong with you?"

He leaned up on his good side so she could see his back.

"Lawd, boy!" she hollered. "You covered in blood. Whip that shirt off right now."

He did. By now the fever had taken him full and his head was floating free like a balloon that had been turned loose. The woman pushed on a few of the slats so that she had better light. She leaned over him and put her face up close to the wound, sniffing.

"I ain't no doctor, son. But I know my menfolk wouldn't leave that untended." She went off in the dark to fetch something. My daddy sat there wishing he could keep all that sorrow pent up, but as much as he wanted to, he just couldn't manage it. It was too much, too heavy with that much pain swelling up inside him like a fist. He sobbed out all of his youngness right there on that stinking floor, wishing to God he had his momma to look after him.

In a few minutes, she come back with a bottle of whiskey and handed it to him to drink. He did so but it came back up as quickly as it went down. She waited another minute while he coughed. Then she told him to brace hisself before she poured a dram over the bullet hole. With the hurt that come on him then, he had to suck down some more to keep his head light. Before long, he was passed out straightaway.

The sleep wasn't restful though. The fever had a real hold on him now. He hollered out at his visions. The woman changed his dressing ever day, pouring that whiskey to keep the wound clean. But she couldn't have known whether he'd make it or die right there in that old house. Just her and him trying to survive in that wrecked place with the war going on all around 'em. It must have been something else.

My daddy once told me that the middle of the night was the only time he come out of those awful dreams. He could behold the starlight and sense the woman there sleeping nearby in the dark, but then he could hear the sounds of cannon over the horizon and it would be so sharp and terrible that he'd wish that fevered dream back on hisself to get away from that real nightmare just an hour's march off.

It was a week before he could stand and walk. He used one of them broke slats for a crutch. It was the smell that drove him to it. The same reek he'd smelt when he first come up to the homeplace. He was still weak, but he knew if he stayed any longer in the foul air, it would undo him. When he finally did manage to hobble out to the fresh air, he was near sun struck. The light just cut right through him, like it was air that had caught fire. He said he never knew the power of all that light that he'd taken for granted until he'd crawled out of that dark place, blind as a stone. Even though it hurt, he made himself stand in the sun until he could feel his body beginning to come back to its shape. The more his mind cleared, the more he could make sense of the body. That was all he needed, he said. From then on, he knew he'd be all right.

He took to sleeping out of doors while he waited to fully mend. The woman, she still stayed in there with that reek, like she was attached to it. Like the smell weren't the issue of some rotten corpse, but the stench of something more terrible. Now that my daddy was recovering, his eyes were fixed a mite better on what sort of woman she was. He heard how she talked to people who weren't there. He noticed the dried stains on her skirts. He knew her heart was good but her head was touched. He sat to figuring as to how he might return the favor of her caring for him. First, though, he needed to know what was so foul inside that damned house. There was no way they could stay much longer in the place. Their provisions had run out. He'd been forced to boil his belt and chew on the leather. All he had left was his shoes, and he didn't know how long he might last if he had to go barefoot in the cold.

He knew the woman could've been a lunatic what had butchered her own mother. There was no telling what sort of things happened when the war moved over people. So he waited for the dead of night and her whispering had hushed before he moved through the house. Even blinded with the dark, he had no trouble following the smell, so overpowering it was. He come into what looked to have once been the kitchen. The roof had come in on itself pretty rough and all the tables and chairs had been smashed, but by the glint of the moon he could make out the fireplace where they had done their roasting. It was in the base of the chimney that he could smell it worst. In the shadows down there he saw a great swell of something moving. Even as a soldier who had looked on war, there was something terrible in what his eyes beheld. It wasn't just one thing moving, but a whole army of something, like rain dribbling down a glass. There were sounds too. Mewing like kittens at the teat.

Now, he didn't know if he was as eager to know what was making them sounds as he had been five minutes earlier. But he figured he'd come further than he should have if he meant to turn a blind eye. So he reached into his shirt pocket for an old Lucifer match and struck it and lit an old piece of candle stub he'd carried in with him for just such a purpose. The flame twisted out and around. He held the candle up.

The roaches, a whole living coat of 'em, they slipped into the shadows. Even that little bit of candle flame was too much for them bugs to bear. They were night creatures, and that appearance of light was God's own unblinking eye on their evil. As they scattered, Daddy could see what had drawn them so. A great lump of flesh and innards. But not that of any breathing body. Instead, it was a mountain of rotted vegetables and fruits of the field, gathered in on top of one another. Some were old and as soft and drawn tight as old skin, but some, some weren't more than a few days out of the ground. But here they were tossed in among all the spoilt food, as poisoned as gunpowder. Daddy told me he could have cried to see so much waste with him being so tight about the belly, but the reek was such that he didn't think on it too much. Instead, he just wadded up some butcher paper from the pantry and set fire to the whole useless mess.

When the flames finally took, the food set to cooking and sputtering. The smell of that burning was fierce, but after the sour green smell of what had been before, it must've been a simple pleasure to have that familiar smell of roasting food crawl up his nose. Seeds burst clear out of pumpkin skins and blackened, smudging the hard brick of the chimney that hadn't seen sign of a cooking fire in some time.

Daddy hadn't had time to ponder what would have caused such a strange gathering of waste before he heard the most God-awful shriek from the other side the kitchen. It was the crazy woman, coming out the shadows, tearing big fistfuls of hair out her own head. She come right at him, bearing down like a witch chasing a soul. If she had scared him that first morning with the shotgun, she coulda yanked his heart right out of his mouth now. Even on the field of battle, he'd never seen such blind hate.

He dodged her and put the old butchering table between him and her so she couldn't get to him. She still growled like some thing born out of the dark. "What has you done!" she finally hollered. "You took it all!"

Daddy had no idea what she was on about. Here he was thinking he'd gotten rid of one hell of a nuisance and she was ready to skin him for it. He'd known her mind wasn't her own, but he'd never suspected such a little bitty gal could have so much meanness in her.

He tried to soothe her, to say it was only rotted plants, but she shoved at the heavy table until she had near pinned him up against the fire he'd started. He could feel the heat of it on the backs of his legs there, like some dog panting at his heels. Heard the sizzle and pop of all of it running to coals. Just as she had him backed up to the flames, the crazy woman's face went as blue-gray as rime frost and she fell face down on the table and went to sobbing like it was the only way to give up the ghost inside her. Daddy watched her shoulders shake, afraid whatever he might do would bring her back to her senses and push him all the way in that hissing fireplace. So he stood still as he could. Waiting while that fire stung the seat of his britches.

"You've taken the food out of my babe's mouth," she moaned. "It was all he had."

Daddy knew good and well that the woman was well past childbearing years and that any babe she spoke of could have been nothing but a spirit of her own devising. Yet there was such sorrow in her plaints that it moved him beyond all reckoning. He come around the edge of the table and laid his hand on her shoulder. He said he felt the weight of her light bones within, as hollow as a sparrow's. She jerked at his touch but she made no move to strike him so he let his hand stay there, steadying her grief.

By and by, Daddy was able to coax her out of the kitchen and out to the moonlit night. She was quieted now but her breathing came in long gasps that fired white blasts of breath into the cold night air. Her eyes seemed as dark as a coal pit.

When he thought the weather had cleared the sorrow from her mind, Daddy led her inside and made up the best pallet he could. He'd forgot his hunger. The site of all that rotted food ablaze must've changed something in the way he thought about living. About what it meant to survive and the price that come of it. All he could think of now was the woman and the pretended death of a child she'd never borne. He knew there was some meaning in it, but it was beyond his ken. She settled down and fell asleep. Daddy watched her for a long time before the tiredness got to be so much that he couldn't help but join her.

In the night she drawed a piece of broke glass across her throat. She hadn't made a sound while the life drained out of her. Daddy had slept right on through the whole thing even though he weren't but on the other side of the room. He buried her that morning out in an old apple orchard and marked her grave with a pile of river rock he fetched up and let dry in the sun. When he finished, he tried to think of some words of the Gospel to put her troubled soul to rest, but Daddy was never much of a hand at learning God's word, so he prayed for her redemption and gathered his pistol and hat and set down the road to rejoin the regiment.

My daddy lived to be forty-two years old. Died in '93. In his whole life, he never did forget what had gotten hold of that woman. He told me it was what became of women in times of war. Why we had to always protect them from it. Their hearts are too tender, he said, to truly know the ways of men. We must remember that the courage a man practices as part of his nature is but a terrible wonder in a woman's eyes. They can never hope to understand the great sacrifice of those who fight for honor.

Now, I've thought about my daddy's words a real long time

and I've realized there's wars both big and small in this world. Not all of them being fought with guns, neither. A man needs to remember his eyes are meant for things a woman's ain't. There might be reason for a woman to lose her senses, but a man is a mirror. The deeper he looks into death, the more he can divide himself from this real world. He is a narrow thing, almost as thin as the place where he can draw into himself where no harm can be done. There's something to be taken from that, with those of you with the ears to listen.

Seven

Hiram slipped out alone late that night after the others had fallen asleep on the cabin's bare floors. He stood under the porch overhang and watched the rain still falling and listened to the horses just a few feet away. Spenser followed. They stood together silently and watched the silver chains of rainwater running off and spiking the loose soil beneath.

"Your daddy sure can tell a war story."

Hiram grunted. "Cause he's never seen one."

Spenser eased his weight onto the porch railing. Hiram brought out his pack of cigarettes, took one himself, and offered another to Spenser without asking if he smoked.

"I hadn't had one since I was over there." Spenser flipped back the creased cover of the matchbook and drew out a match with a gesture as deliberate as a seamstress with a needle.

"Never known a man that soldiered that would decline a smoke."

"No, I guess I haven't either."

They talked of the rain and when it might abate. Neither believed it would last much longer. Soon they would have to rejoin the trail. What that might mean, they conceded, was still unknown.

"Those boys in there, they sure thought a heap of that story, didn't they?" Hiram said. "Hell, I've never seen boys that age that won't shut up when some old fool starts barking about cannon fire." He felt his voice had grown too loud and he looked out at the dark and shook his head. "You know what he says about never going off to war himself? He thinks he's been cheated by God. Said so to my mama one time. Her with a dead young'un on her hands because he went off and got him shot and that's what he says to her. Cheated by God. I'm guessing you already know about my brother. Everybody around here does, I imagine."

Spenser nodded. "Hell of a thing." The cigarette tip glowed up on his face like a collapsing sun. "Fathers are hard. Every one of them is God in his boy's eyes. My father, he never pretended to know anything about what it meant to serve in the army. But that didn't matter. When I got back he couldn't understand why I wouldn't sit around the fireplace and fill him full of stories of the great campaign. Thought something was wrong with me for not wanting to talk about it."

"You were an officer, weren't you?"

Spenser smiled and shook his head. "Hell, no. I was a buck private. Thought it would be more glorious to serve beside the common man. Thought that's how you got the true flavor of experience."

"Boy, I bet I know what flavor that was."

They laughed together and let the downpour do its worst. In a few hours they had talked through the last remnants of the storm and listened to the gentle pattering of the raindrops blown clear in rallying wind gusts. Knowing the day would soon be on them, they said their good nights and crept back inside to find some place in the cabin to get what sleep they could before it was time to set out.

Hiram woke to a rough prod in his shoulder. He opened his eyes to see Sloane standing over him, a broad-brimmed hat clapped to his head. When he remained on the floor, he felt the prod again, the unmistakably sharp toe of a boot. Sloane's voice fell from the dark. "You ain't no better about getting up now than when you was a little boy."

That was enough to rouse Hiram. He blinked and looked around. None of the others had yet been disturbed. Their gentle snores played a rough harmonic in the cabin.

Hiram got the fire going in the wood stove and set the coffee pot to boil while Sloane shook the other men awake. While they stretched and yawned and stamped the heavy sleep off of them, Sloane came up to the kitchen and sat at the table to watch over his son's shoulder.

"I guess this means you've decided to come along. I still don't know how you'll manage to get along with that gimp of yours."

Sloane did not answer, but hauled his leather possibles bag from around his neck and laid it on the table before him. He opened the flap and drew out the old Dragoon pistol and removed the cylinder, pulling the old balls, patches, and powder, the loose grains running out as soft as sand onto the raw pine tabletop. He then set the cylinder on its end and removed the small percussion caps and swept the ballistic materials into the palm of his hand and dumped them in a wastebasket at his feet. He eased the cylinder back into its mounting and linched it in place, turning it with the steady clicks to ensure it seated properly. Satisfied that it was, he poured out a fresh measure of powder and followed it with an oiled patch and ball and snugged it in the cylinder with a firm tug back on the loading bar. When he had loaded all six bored slots and fitted the caps to each shot nipple, Hiram had the coffee ready and the old man put the pistol away.

Sheriff Painter crossed the front room, hocking up a silvery oyster of early morning phlegm as he opened the front door and spat into the darkness beyond. He crowed appreciatively at the sight of no more rain while he dragged his fingers across his vast belly. The Price brothers, addled from their first genuine hangover, did not suffer the sheriff's optimism gladly. They poked at their boots and clumped into the kitchen for a mug of something hot. Hiram served the coffee and had them wait a few more minutes while the eggs boiled.

Once they had eaten, they collected their rifles and went outside to see about the horses. The animals shuffled against one another, stamping and swinging their heavy bodies in agitation. Every man quickly worked at breaking down the canvas shelter and stowing the separate pieces in their respective saddlebags. It grew light, but with the overcast still lingering there was no sun. They rode away from the cabin under a sky the color and heft of stone.

Sloane rode double with Johnson Price. Sheriff Painter rode just behind. The old man acted as guide, taking them up past a dead grove of blackened hardwoods that had burned one distant summer during a wildfire. Though it had stopped raining, the water in the river was higher now than when Hiram had led the nighttime crossing. They needed to get to the lowest ford they could before cutting a decent trail for the abandoned hunting camp.

Noon found them still paralleling the stream. Hiram rode up to the front of the march and asked his father if he knew how far the ford might be. Sloane did not look at his son. Instead, he turned his head toward the sheriff and assured him it was not much further yet.

The first attempt to cross was above a dislodged beaver dam. The floodwaters boiled and carved a smooth flowing slide over the wrenched logs and submerged terrain. Spenser and Hiram sat their horses beside one another high up on the bank and watched Macon Price venture out. The boy quailed as soon as he felt the strength of the current and he struggled back to solid ground. Hiram shook his head and they kept moving further upstream.

They tried again at a stretch of granite flats, but it proved too slick. Sheriff Painter cursed. Sloane sat looking silently on.

With the day done and the men and horses exhausted, the sheriff agreed to have the men encamp for the night and wait for the waters to recede. They managed to find some good high ground that had drained well during the day. They stripped kindling from the bark of cedar trees, dragging out long thin curls of wood from the trunks with their hunting knives. Once they carefully set the shavings and erected a small temple of deadfall branches, they were able to coerce a steady flame, feeding larger sticks while they dried heavier logs in a nearby pile.

After they had eaten what little they still had in their private stores, they sat and watched the flames wrung out by the wind. Hiram decided it was time to tell his story.

All those sitting around the fire, even Sloane, were content to listen.

This is my mama's story, but I remember it well enough.

Her granddaddy was a man by the name of Albion McKinney. I'm no professor at family history, but his name was one she always made sure I knew. He came down from a long line of Scots-Irish that had headed south through the Cumberland Gap to find peace in these mountains. They came down poor and they stayed poor, but there wasn't a lazy hand among them. They farmed and traded and begot their families with the endurance of people with nothing to depend on for their living but what they could scratch out of the ground themselves.

Albion's wife was a Pentecostal woman from Tennessee named Mary Beck. She was good-looking and a bit above her husband socially, but that was the pairing designed by some hand neither of them rightly understood. It was as though their life together was just plain ordained and that was the beginning and ending of it.

They wasted no time in their Biblical begetting. Three summers later they had three little ones, the last of them being my mother's aunt Beth born in 1859. It was hardscrabble going for the young family. Ole Albion turned his hand at raising tobacco but he had a run of bad weather and worse rates of exchange. Mary bore up under it as well as she could. She knew Albion was too proud a man to go to his in-laws for handouts, no matter how rough the going got to be, so she always made sure the young'uns were fixed up as well as they could be whenever it was time to pay the Becks a visit.

But if it was hard before, it grew all the more trying in the late summer of 1860. One day while he was out in the tobacco patch working at suckering his plants, Albion was struck full on with the spirit. He fell down in his rows and lay there with his eyes at the overhead sun, his legs still kicking. When he came to he remembered God himself coming down to talk him through the fit. Albion was so moved by it, he decided right there and then that he needed to found his own church to commemorate God's goodness.

He ran straight home to tell Mary what had happened. She may well have suspected the heat had gotten to him, but if so, she held her tongue for the moment. What was a young wife to make of her man raving about the vision of God in his own backyard, even if she walked in the bright heights of God's church presence every Sunday?

Now, poor crop yields aside, that patch of tobacco looked to turn a better profit than the building of a church house. While Albion busied himself with sketches and long afternoon surveys of nearby pastures in his search for a proper building ground, Mary saw to the raising of those crops. She'd take her children out there right in the middle of those blistering rows and turn her hand at farming and child rearing, each in its turn.

Albion did not stop to think what he was asking of this good woman. He was full up with the spirit, and when a man is hellbent like that, there ain't much you can do to turn his will aside. The first convert was the old widow who'd let him build on her place. By the end of that first summer he had enough voices lifted in hallelujahs that the cabin joists were shaking and popping against that tin roof whenever he shouted for an amen.

Well, war went and broke out and though it hadn't yet reached the hill country, there was a great deal of talk among the locals. Things being what they were, it wasn't long before a call went up to the mountain people to organize themselves into formal companies of militia in order to join the Southern cause. Now that the order had been officially issued, men took to arms pretty quick. Albion, though, being a man guided by his personal vision of the Lord, wasn't so quick to join the fray. He prayed on it for most of a week. Members of the congregation waited to hear what he would say.

When that fateful Sunday arrived, Albion climbed up into his little pulpit and leaned forward, looking out at the room full of sunburned faces. Most had been there since a little before dawn to make sure they had a spot of pew to sit on. Those that hadn't been up with the chickens had to stand out in the yard to listen. The front doors had to be propped open and the single window had the glass up so all those outside could hear what Albion had to say.

He closed the Bible lying on the rostrum. He knew the words he needed to say would not be printed in any book, even a holy one. He cleared his throat and began talking. It was the story of Cain and Abel.

Now, he conjured the story in ways no Bible verse ever had. Each man, woman and child sitting in that room could swear the sweetest smells of a perfect world wafted right on through that church house. The beauty of all that ancient goodness was as clear as a picture book. The ancient brothers themselves, they were as much flesh and blood as if they were your very neighbors. There was nothing highfalutin in that old story, and it meant all the more just because that was how he told it. When it came to the murder, ole Albion made them see the treachery and the blood pouring forth from the fatal wound. The wound of one brother to another, proof of a terrible and final shame. Half of the congregation was quick to shout out their amens. The others were out the door before he could speak the words of the benediction.

That next week talk got around. Men said that the preacher had stepped beyond his office in making the pulpit a place for his opinions about the war, that he'd wrung up the word of God to his own ends. Others said it was a true disciple's duty to live by the scripture as he saw best.

The men who were of a mind drummed up support for the militia company. In not more than a couple of weeks, they had a smart file of men ready to seek the adventure the Confederate army had to offer them. When they marched off there was a whole gathering of womenfolk singing ditties about the honor and courage of their men. But none of those that listened to Albion's preaching had to suffer that bitter parting. They tricked themselves into thinking the war didn't concern them, though they were soon to learn otherwise.

The little church house filled once more, and he continued to preach the love and forgiveness needed to redeem the world.

This passed for a time. The mountains were a long way from the battles in Virginia. The only news they heard of their men came in the occasional letter or newspaper clipping. None of the men had perished in the line of duty that first winter, so it was possible for the women to pray and hope for some unselfish miracle of all the boys coming home to the hills.

Early the next spring, when the season for warring had come back around and the mountain snows had melted down to rock and mud, a group of riders appeared. They were rough looking men with dirty beards and patchworked uniforms. They wore braided symbols of rank, but looked nothing like any army the villagers had ever seen or even imagined. They called themselves deputies of the North Carolina home guard and appointed themselves as the force of law and order in the highland country. Their leader was a man by the name of Blount. Called himself a lieutenant colonel, though the likelihood of that commission being formalized in anything other than his own mind is passing unlikely.

The riders claimed they had word of deserters holed up in and about the area. Now, there had been no such sightings as far as any of the townsfolk knew of, but they understood from the beginning that Blount would take their assurance as worthless. It was plain he and his men intended to make themselves a fixture about the hills as long as most of the young and strong were away fighting. There are more than one kind of spoils in times of war and more than one kind of spoiler. Blount was reckoned to be a dangerous animal once caged, now let loose to roam at his will. Most decided the best way to deal with him was by giving him handouts, keeping he and his men drunk and stuffed with food. The only thing worse than a wild animal freed is one that was starved down to desperation. So the villagers carried out the best of their laid-by stores and entertained Blount's company of outliers to keep his outrage quieted. For a time, it worked.

Albion continued holding services. He didn't alter his sermons one whit. He felt the conviction of the Lord's own words lying like a weight upon his shoulders. He would not repeat the sin of Jonah. He would not keep the burden of truth to himself when he knew the congregation needed it more than ever.

Mary feared for her husband. With three small children entrusted to her care, she did not enjoy the idealism that drove Albion. She saw that it was only a matter of time before his acts would cause awful consequences to their world.

It happened midsummer. A small group of Blount's men staggered drunk into the evening service. They laughed and belched and showed every rotten behavior you could imagine while Albion read a homily. The villagers in attendance were mostly old men and women. They didn't dare turn around and hush the newcomers. They just closed their eyes and pinned their minds to the words Albion was speaking. But the men kept at it, laughing loud and toasting one another with tin cups of whiskey under God's own roof.

Finally, ole Albion had enough of it. He leapt out from behind that pulpit with his Bible waving in front of him like a black wing of some bird meant to fly straight at evil. He wasn't little timid Albion anymore, but a prophet of rage let loose on these wolves running amid his flock. He came at them shouting, "Is it not written," he hollered. "Is it not written, 'My house shall be called of all nations the house of prayer'? But ye have made it a den of thieves!"

The men were not expecting the wrath the skinny preacher threw at them, finding themselves stunned silent. They knew well enough how to fight back against a man with vulgar curses, but a helping of fire-tongued scripture was beyond them. They got to their feet and shuffled out. But the door closing behind them wasn't the last of the story.

Three days later, Colonel Blount rode up to Albion's place and hollered for him to come out or he'd light fire to the cabin's very foundations. Mary begged Albion to hide and pretend he was away on some circuit preaching, but my mama's granddaddy knew things had gone too far to hide behind lies and his wife's skirts. He stepped right on out there onto the porch and looked Blount eye to eye, for the colonel hadn't even bothered getting down from his horse.

That dirty bushwhacker sat right there and told Albion he considered every man able to walk without the aid of a cane fit for service and therefore a likely deserter from Jeff Davis' army. He said he was willing to extend clemency to all those scoundrels about the region if they mustered themselves the following afternoon on the village green. Any able-bodied man not mustered and later found about the territory would be subject to immediate execution by firing squad. He then turned his big black horse with a sharp yell back down the mountain, his lieutenants following at his heels.

Albion knew he had little time. He saddled his poor broken-down nag and told Mary to take the children up to her mother's place. She refused at first, feeling it was only right to stand her husband in good stead in this moment of crisis. But she realized too that danger was now bearing down on all their lives and it was her sacred duty to tend to their children. So she gathered what few things they could carry and wrapped them in an old quilt, and they set off for the full half-week's march to find her family's home. My mother's aunt Beth, she was only three years old at the time, but Mary could carry her for only so far. The rest, that little girl had to walk herself.

It was an ordeal all right. Mary had to tug and pet those little children, the oldest one only seven years old, to get them through those woods. All the while, she feared the sound of hoofbeats on the earth. If Blount and his men knew the preacher's wife was in flight there was no telling what vengeance they might exact. Mary knew that desperate men were capable of any manner of evil.

Blistered and bloodied, they stopped only for a few hours during the night and slept huddled together without the benefit of a campfire. There was too much to lose if they were caught, and the light and smell of a fire was too much to risk. The children moaned and cried and Mary did her best to lullaby it all away.

Albion must have worried over his young family, but he had no time to dwell on them now. While Mary and the children fled to what they believed to be safer ground, the preacher rode to every family within the territory, passing the word to the men to ride up to the top ridge that night. Before they had time to ask what was the matter, he drove his heels into the horse's flanks to reach the next household as fast as he could. Once he'd made the full circuit, he rode up to the ridge himself and sat his horse in a full lather under the moon, waiting for the other men to join him.

In time, they came. Walking their horses and mules into the clearing in twos and threes, they didn't make much noise. They only nodded their greetings to one another and kept their faces behind the low brims of their hats. They knew something had befallen that didn't call for easy talk. Some chewed tobacco and smoked pipes, but no one brought a cup of whiskey.

Albion spoke to them in a whisper, telling them he intended to fight the outliers, every single one, until they could make no demands on the men of the hill country. They cast straws to see how many would join. Albion passed his hat and turned his back while the men voted. When it came back around he had his answer. Not a single one shirked. He told the men to ride back to their families that night and send them away to kinfolk who could keep them safe. They would have to be quick because as soon as daybreak they would find themselves men with a price on their head.

They agreed to meet on that same ridge in three nights. It was enough time to see their women and children carried away. That was all they were granted before it was agreed they start their warring. The weather was kind to them. It rained hard, keeping Blount's men warm and drunk indoors. By the time it let up, every cabin in the area stood empty.

Blount was furious once he found out. He had his men fire the cabins. So many burned that first night, I've heard it said a man could see a ground glow as far away as Tennessee. It was all wasted spite though. The men who watched their homes burn did not think of the loss to themselves and their families. Instead, it only proved Albion right that Blount's people were no better than criminals themselves. From that moment on, the preacher's army never suffered from the first lick of insubordination. They all had a common enemy now, and a common cause.

For the next several months Albion's riders kept to the highest hills. They made their campfires in cairns, careful to make sure they never gave Blount's scouts the first sign of their movement. They ate only what they could take off the land, and they learned to do well enough with whatever God allowed them. Any man who complained was hushed by the looks his comrades gave him. It wasn't as if every one of them, Albion included, didn't suffer the same.

They raided Blount only at night. Because they knew the country so well, they could cross the clearings and attack before the guardsmen had time to throw up a good defense. Often, it wasn't much more than a light skirmish and Albion's men would be away in as many directions as there were riders, raising a war whoop that echoed all about. The guardsmen would give pursuit, but there was no use. There was no way to track the movement of so many ghosts in the dark.

The casualties began to mount. But not in the way you might think. It wasn't the loss of blood that was the concern, but morale. Albion's men were quick in their raids, but their aim was hurried and wild. An attack rarely did more than frighten Blount's soldiers. Only two men had been shot in an entire season of the night attacks and one of those may well have been from the barrel of a friendly pistol fired in the middle of all that midnight confusion.

But be that as it may, it was taking a toll. The men weren't sleeping and they began to ask Blount questions, such as why they didn't move on to another spot of country that didn't offer the perils of the highlands. Now, being a man of quick temper, you can imagine he wasn't at all pleased with this turn of events. He threatened to shoot the next man that suggested they leave off the war they'd gotten themselves into, and said any such talk was no better than out and out mutiny.

He tried sending night parties out himself to find where Albion's men kept themselves, but they always came back on exhausted horses saying they'd found nothing but a whole world of empty mountain dark. They said going out there was like being swallowed. Blount raged and fumed, but no matter how hard he drove his guardsmen, they could no more find where Albion kept his army than they could walk across water.

It was then that Blount had his idea to take the war to a different quarter. He knew there was no way women and children could be as slippery as the men who rode the ridges. The helpless would have had to have been sent away. The question was where. Blount put his old ear to the ground and found out. Found out too what had become of Albion's wife and children and he made plans to take out his vengeance there since Albion refused to make himself a target. At the time, though, no one could have guessed what he had in mind.

Now, Mary had managed in her time at her parents' house to cut out a slice of home for herself and her children. She had not heard the first word from Albion since he sent her off and in his absence she'd had to make the best of the place she found herself in. Her momma had let her plant her own vegetable garden in the side yard so that she could drag out some kind of independent living. The Becks had even emptied out an entire wing of the homeplace so that she could make a house within the house, a spot where it was only her and her babies without having to feel she was once more dependent on the folks who had raised her. But while the Becks were understanding people, it was hard going. Mary's oldest child was only seven years old. That was the boy Mattie. It was my grandma Sarah that was the middle child. And my great-aunt Beth was the littlest, still not even talking in true sentences yet.

Now, Mattie had taken it on himself to act the man of the family since his daddy was off fighting. Mary hadn't thought to make much of it as it seemed to help the boy feel better about the situation by taking over as he thought a proper young man should. He worked hard in the fields, dragging turnips up out of the ground even once the sun had gone down and his momma had called him in for supper. He must have felt each blister and ache he earned justified his rank. As the boy, he must have thought suffering and being in charge of things had something to do with one another.

It was a hot day with the threat of storm clouds and Mary had brought Sarah and Beth in from the fields because she was afraid of having them fall sunstruck. She had felt ill herself and knew it was only a matter of time before the weather got to the children as well. She made them sit still in the shade of the big house and went to the kitchen to pour out glasses of lemonade. She'd told Mattie to come in as well, but he remained as stubborn as ever. Her parents were sitting out on the front porch taking what breeze they could. They could see the garden where Mattie worked, so Mary didn't worry too much about the boy. His grandparents would give a holler if he needed attention.

Well, she took the lemonade back to the little girls and they all sat there sipping at it. Mary pressed the glass to the side of her face to soak away the fever in her skin. She couldn't remember it ever being so hot, not even when she was a very little girl. But being back in the cool of the house made it better. It was so far back that the outside sounds were faint and pitched different than what she was used to hearing. It was like listening to the outside world from the bottom of a deep well. That's why she didn't know what to make of the shouting at first, racketing at it did through all the house's nooks and turns.

Mary told the girls to keep still while she saw what was the matter. When she got up to the front of the house she could see a group of Blount's guardsmen had ridden up to the side yard and were talking to the Becks. Mattie was still out in the garden not saying anything but standing with his hands on his hips and squinting up at them. Mary knew that she needed to get back to the girls before they figured out what was going on. She crept to the back of the house and told the little girls to be as quiet as ever they could be, because they were going to play a sneaking game against their grandparents and older brother. Being little bitty gals, they took her at her word and all three slipped out quiet as their own shadows through the back door and into the woods.

Mary took them on up the hill through the thickest places she could find, lifting away briars so they wouldn't be pricked and cry out. Finally, she settled in among some blueberry vines and said that they had to be as still as they could until she came back for them. The sisters, still as sure as ever this was the finest game they'd ever heard of, giggled and nodded their heads.

She came back down the hill and circled behind some mountain laurel to see what was happening. Some of the guardsmen had dismounted from their horses and were walking toward the house. She could hear them knocking things over inside, maybe looking for her and the girls or maybe just breaking things to frighten the Becks. Blount still sat on his horse. He was leaning so far forward in his saddle that it looked his head was joined at the neck with the beast. He was talking to Mary's daddy, saying something that Mary tried her best to hear but couldn't.

It happened fast after that. Two of the men took Mattie by the shoulders and forced him up against a forked locust tree, tying his arms with strips of old rawhide. He bucked and yelled. Not like a little boy frightened, but an angry man trapped inside a young'un's body. Mary didn't even realize she was coming down the mountain, running as fast as she could. She could see only the woods whirl around her as she tried to bridge the gap between her and her boy.

Her father had made to free his grandchild, crossing the yard in long strides. Just as he raised his hand to loosen the boy's binding, Blount raised his pistol and fired a ball through the old man's temple.

As old man Beck fell to the ground, so did Mary. She had her breath bled right out. A silent moment followed before Mrs. Beck raised her voice in the fiercest mourning you could imagine. The boy Mattie just looked on, his face peppered with his granddaddy's gore.

The other guardsmen, they were as shocked as anyone. They had no idea murder was the plan of the afternoon, and it only just starting.

It wasn't long before Blount turned around and called out Mary's name. He said if she came down and told him where Albion was, she and her family would be spared. If not, that day would go on for a million years. Mary knew it was a lie and that as soon as she gave herself and the girls away they were as good as dead. Men like Blount wouldn't be satisfied their brand of work was done until there were none left.

Even so, when they went to cutting on Mattie, she was about to give herself up anyway. The boy's screams were something awful for a mother to have to bear. His little arms laid open like a rabbit's hide, she was about the step into the clearing when her own mother rose up from the sobbing heap she'd been and charged at Blount, flailing open handed blows in his general direction. He stepped to the side and slammed the heavy butt of his horse pistol down on her skull. She went down like a stone. To make sure it was enough, one of the guardsmen fired his carbine into her throat. Her blood ran dark onto the dark ground.

Mary heard something behind her. She knew she had come too close, had likely been seen by the outliers. She knew there was nothing she could do to stop them. Her whole life was being ripped away and she had no power to counter it. Albion's God was not in the woods with her that day. Whatever was had a power she couldn't imagine. She just wanted to be taken up and crushed in its jaws. Let the evil digest her whole. Anything to keep her from this kind of pain.

The steps came closer and she could sense someone standing within arm's reach. Then she felt the touch against her shoulder and her daughter Sarah's soft voice asking if the game was over yet. She immediately drew the little girl to her chest, burying her face there so she couldn't see what had happened below. She told her to hush, that they might still win yet.

Mary carried her back uphill, moving as quietly through the leaves and underbrush as she could. The touch of her little girl had told her something. No matter what outrage Blount and his men would commit, she could not giver her daughters over to it as well. They had to survive. And she would have to live with whatever she knew to make sure they did.

Once back in their hidey-hole, Mary told them to cover their ears and close their eyes, that pretending they were invisible might make them so. How she must have wished she had done the same herself, but Mary was a strong woman and she wouldn't pardon herself from the grief of hearing what they were doing to the boy. Heard Blount too yelling out that it would all stop if she would only bring herself and the little girls out. But she forced herself not to move.

It was late, almost on to sunset, when Blount and his men

fired the homeplace and rode out. Once she was sure they were clear, Mary went down to her dead child but she didn't cry or holler out. Who knows why? Maybe it was because the unrealness of it made it somehow more bearable. She had only heard of such things as this in the Bible. Maybe she felt like looking at her boy was like hearing one of the old stories of men laid to ruin by the hand of a vengeful God. Time had come loose from where it was supposed to stay, and all that mattered now was that her boy's blood was on the ground. How would crying be big enough to explain that?

She went up to him and untied his hands, catching his weight when he slumped forward. She laid his body carefully out on the ground. Mattie looked not like a boy, but an animal about to be gut-stripped. His mouth had been stoppered with pinecones to muffle his screams while the butchers had worked on him. The skin on his arms and legs had been peeled away so that the raw muscle showed through. There was a strange glow to the exposed flesh, as if his body had a lamp within that wouldn't snuff itself even though life was gone.

By now the girls had gotten impatient and scared from hearing the house burn. They had come into the yard and when they saw their mother bent over their murdered brother, they set to keening. Mary didn't have to do more than look over at them and tell them to hush before they quieted. They must have seen something in her face. She was still their mother, but the world was different now. They'd hidden because they believed it had been a game, but now they understood even games could be counterfeits of themselves. Their hiding had saved them, yes. But in saving them it had robbed their lives of anything dependable, knowable.

That night Mary and the girls worked by the light of the burning house. While the girls washed the bodies of the Becks and

Mattie, Mary dug one grave in the softest ground she could find, prying up stones and knobby roots, working as hard as any man. It took all of the night and into the morning before the hole was drawn out deep and wide. She told the little girls to pray for her strength and while they did she grabbed her daddy by his ankles and dragged him across the yard. He was heavy but once she let him slide from the rim of the earth down into the grave she knew the others would go easy. That, at least, was a grace.

Once they were all in the ground together, Mary let the little girls take turns shoveling the loose dirt over them. She said it was important that it be done well and proper and that meant all of them should take a hand in their burying. Family deserved that.

It was a week before Albion found them living in the burned-out skeleton of the old homeplace. Some miracle of the fire's path left enough to keep them sheltered from the weather and they'd made a new home among the wreckage. When he came to his son's grave, he fell to his knees and cursed God for taking so much from him. But Mary took her husband's hand and told him to bring no more evil down on their heads and made him beg the Lord's forgiveness. He was a humble man, so he listened to her.

There was no more warring after that. Maybe some men would have put themselves on a road to vengeance, gone after Blount and his men. But Mary told Albion that all the killing he might do would not bring their boy back from the dead. They had a family to tend, and she needed him to be a father now, not a soldier.

My momma told me a little bit of what her grandma Mary was like. She was a tall woman with long hair that was still pretty and full even when it'd gone full white from old age. Old Albion was dead by then, carried off by a weak heart after he'd helped Mary raise those two little girls to marrying age. But Mary lived long enough to see both those children of hers bring their own offspring into the world. I was the last of the ones born she laid hands on. My momma said it was important to her that Mary knew I was alive and well, a little boy brought to the family all those years later because of what she had to endure.

Now, that's the God's truth. That's the burden that woman shouldered her whole long life. I think that takes something. I guess I'd like to know what it is or was, but I'm not pinning my hope to it. There are just some things that a man might come to know, but which he'll never be able to say.

Eight

While the other men were still sleeping, Sloane watched a doe and fawn working along the eastern ridge overlooking the camp, a brass band of dawn seeping faintly at the horizon. Without making a sound, the old man moved out into the still-dark clearing bent as low as his back would allow, his left shoulder hitched up high against the pain needling his spine. The pain was from no new injury. It had been there with him for years, always as close as breath. But now it was worse.

After walking a while, he grew tired in his limbs and stopped and hid himself among the few patches of tall sedge and cleaver. He carried his old pistol. It was just an easy habit in his hands, not a piece of iron designed to kill. But the weight felt good all the same.

He didn't know what had drawn him to follow the deer. He had been lying by the whispering coals of the fire in that sleeplessness old men know so well. Then some sense brought him out, an awareness of game on the move. It was something he'd once tried to explain to Hiram long ago.

This faith in a notion, as brief and thin as smoke, but still something you couldn't deny. A knowing that the animals were trying to slip past without actually seeing or hearing or even smelling them. Like they were creatures of your own imagining and obedient to your wakened and curious will. The quiet certainty. That was so much more powerful than the killing. So much closer to what life as a man was truly about. And it was sealed in your mind and heart long before you ever touched your finger to the trigger.

The deer moved slow as fog across the ridge, their muzzles alternately dipping for acorns and testing the air for the scent of predators, but the wind was coming high off the mountain faces across the valley and all they could drink into their working nostrils was rivers of empty air. Sloane crept forward once more, having no idea at all what he hoped to do by bringing himself closer to them, but moving with intent and time-honed skill.

And then somehow they knew he was there. In that same magic vapor that alerted men to beasts, so too could animals sense men without a betraying scent or cracked twig. The doe's ears snapped up high and swiveled at the base of her skull, probing the space around her for the proof that would justify her taut nerves. The fawn too held its slender neck erect, staring out of its own bound fright, ready to terrify itself into muscular action. Sloane stood still. These were the moments that decided everything, Sloane knew. Whatever happened next would cast all the danger and care and instinct and inborn luck aside. None of that would matter once the animal took its measure of the man and the man bore it.

The doe snorted and tossed her tail high. Together, she and the fawn vanished into the greater wilderness. Sloane stood there studying the place of their going before he collected himself and edged his way back to camp.

The Price boys were awake and had a fire built. Its flames wavered up, bending the air above like a piece of distorted mirroring. Sloane came close to the fire and bent over at the waist and put his bare hands out to warm his palms. His body felt cold in its extremities though he knew it was another summer morning and really not that cold at all. But the cold was like the pain. There were times when that's all there was.

Hiram came back from watering the horses. His uniform jacket was all buttoned up and his felt hat set at the strict military angle. How had the boy Sloane raised become such a creature of habit?

Sloane ventured a word. "I think we might make a crossing today."

Hiram squatted down to where the mess tins had been set out for the fire and cracked open one of the jars of beans. "You think so, huh?"

"I figure there's a good spot about three miles up the pocket of this here ridge that tails down to the water. Old slides through there if memory serves. Should make for an even ford. Nice smooth water and a firm bottom. Once we get through there it shouldn't be but about a couple hours down to the old camp."

Hiram spread the bean paste out in the pan and stirred in a stiff pat of butter that sizzled when he held the skillet over the flames. "Should have been in there by yesterday. God knows where that crazy old man's taken her by now."

Sloane settled onto a rounded stone on a little ledge overlooking the valley. The forest floor below was coming up gradually from its distant blue sleep, the contours of the earth sliding out from the nighttime shadows like a pall prematurely drawn. The sun's bull neck was just above the spraddled mountains.

"I don't reckon old Matt means to do much running. He's about busted up in body as me. Surely he don't mean to keep ahead of no posse."

"Well, we'll see, I guess."

They got going before long, Sheriff Painter saying he had a good feeling that justice would be met this day and all their labors would be brought to a moral end. No one bothered to contradict the sheriff, but Sloane could feel the eyes of Hiram and the judge's boy fixed hard on his and the sheriff's backs. He wanted to face them and have them come out and say what they thought. He hated their silence. Especially Hiram's. Him a crippled up old man reduced to riding double with this Price boy and them still young and proud, but expecting him to show them the way up to this deserted camp. A place broken and already mostly gone back to earth. Maybe they believed only a man in like condition could know the way to such a collapsed place. He leaned from the saddle and spat.

He was right about the crossing. The waters had receded and the horses could make their way over the pebbled bottom easily enough, the sun high and pleasant because of the cross breeze. It was the first stroke of luck he'd had. It made no sense that it had been so hard finding a way over. Sloane knew the woods well. He'd never laid a foot beyond the mountains, and in keeping himself in this one patch of the world, he had come to comprehend it as closely as a man possibly could. When it concerned the woods, he simply did not make mistakes. But with Hiram back every decision he made, every instinct he followed, seemed to bear false.

He wondered if when his son had returned he'd brought something more than his body and his hate. Perhaps some of that old misfortune came too, like a returning fever or a criminal long restless for bloodshed.

They came into the abandoned camp not much before noon. Hiram, the judge's son, and Sheriff Painter rode up in front now, splitting off in different directions to scout the periphery of the battered outbuildings, little rectangles of pressboard and sheets of skewed tin. Sloane and the Price brothers sat and watched.

Painter got down off his horse and lumbered over to where an extinguished smudge fire blackened a circle under one of the sheets of tin. He eased down on popping joints and looked to see what might be left of Matt Vaughn's going. With his index finger he drew a stripe through the soot. The sheriff stood. "Sometime this morning."

Spenser and Hiram checked the trails leading in and out, looking for tracks. Hiram was the one who found sign first and called the others. They rode to the sound of his voice and then followed the march of the others as they moved down a flat of blighted and branch tangled longleaf pine. As the Price boy rode the horse down, Sloane braced himself against his body's ache and leaned from the saddle to better see where the hoof marks had stamped red sickles in the red mud. They'd been laid at a trot.

It wasn't long before they came upon the crows. Three of them strung along the span of a dead poplar limb. A leafy green vine thick and milky and unbruised wound around the tree's guttered trunk. It, and the crows themselves, were the only things alive in that little hollow. For a great distance, all they could see was stunted mixed hardwoods carried off by blight, rotting where they stood in various stages of decay. Some few larger trees had already been felled by winds that would have had to shoot clean through the gap. Their exposed root systems thrust dozens of accusing fingers.

But what chilled Sloane was the impossibility of the crows. The strained sound of their croaking drawn out thin and sharp and brooding. And then the movement in their swollen throats, as if their bodies strove to capture the sound born premature from their mouths, already loosed into the air though the birds had not exercised their fluted muscles to shape note and voice. The sound and then the throat's movement to deliver that sound. Not the delay between seeing a thing from a distance and then waiting to hear the report, a well-tuned law of space and physics. But that law collapsed, corrupted in the lawlessness of that dead hollow, sound outside of time and contemptuous of it, allowing for things that could not be happening as they were even though they were. Worse than a dark hallucination, because it was shared and beyond arguing. Something was happening down there that only a truly mad man could accept.

Hiram nudged his horse and spoke it forward. The gray stamped and did not move and none of the other horsemen tried to do the same with their mounts, all gone still and silent, horses and men alike. Hiram spoke again and this time the horse obeyed, leading him alone down toward the dead poplar. Sloane, along with the Price boy holding the reins, sat where they were and watched.

The crows quieted and waddled back and forth, squat and petulant, snapping their gold eyes at one another before Hiram drew so close that they took wing and passed over the ridge. Once they had gone, the judge's son and the others put their horses forward, following Hiram on in.

Sloane let his eyes wander the tree's skeletons. What lay ahead could be nothing any of them would wish to see. This was already something beyond what Sloane knew or wanted to know. Him with all these years among the hill country and to discover something like this, terrible not just in its novelty but in its nativity, fixed here for who knew how long and yet hidden from his eyes. A square patch of something evil in his own homeland and him as blind to it as a copperhead at the rising of the Dog Star. And how strange that his son would ride straight into it, like he was born equal to whatever might wait out there to savage him.

When Hiram stopped, the others did as well, not needing to hear a shout of warning, all as nervy and spooked as the animals they rode. Sloane could not see well for the broad back of the Price boy, but as the horse beneath them shied and turned, he saw a glimpse of something white and hunched. Painter muttered something to the judge's son who only nodded and sat up straight in his saddle, his big, gloved hand furtively working to free his rifle from its lashings.

The sheriff turned his head toward Sloane. "So I guess this would be the time to say something to him, Mr. Tobit."

Sloane still could not see well. He had to get down, to feel the stiffness of the land beneath him. The horse ride had been too much. Tiredness flooded up in him and he felt if he closed his eyes he might completely lose his balance and topple. The Price boy dismounted first and then helped Sloane to the ground, using his shoulder to steady him on the way down. Sloane thanked him and limped forward.

In the gray and tangled and vine hanging-wood there was a clearing. Sunlight blanched it like scalded hide. In the midst of the patch of weird light, squatted toadlike on a planed stump, the old man Matt Vaughn was whispering something. His arms were black to the elbow with blood, his pale trunk and naked thighs dappled with the same, but the blood came from no injury on his body. Sloane knew then that the girl was dead.

Sloane spoke Vaughn's name and then his own but Vaughn showed no recognition of either who he was or who had come to collect him. Hiram rode back to speak with the sheriff.

While the others quietly discussed what should be done, Sloane eased himself onto another leveled stump not far from Vaughn. He wondered if this whole valley had been clear cut just to give tired old men a place to sit.

He looked at Vaughn. What was this thing he was seeing? Not the man he knew, but the shape of him distorted by an imploded nothing. Hell or something more than that locked within a human skull. Each of them had slain their children. But why had Sloane been able to survive the killing of his boy with his eyes still clear, unclouded by the comfort of madness? Why had God allowed that? And it an accident, a drunken mistake. But what Vaughn had done was something beyond the error of a fool because at least a fool could be comprehended. A world made up of sins and burdens. Vaughn was proof of something beyond those reckonings. This was not only death, this was a thing unnatural. This was without cause. What were you to do when even evil fled? What could you bring yourself to hate if not that?

Hiram and the judge's son said they would go on to find the girl's body. The oldest Price boy said he'd go along too, but Hiram refused and rode over the hillcrest before any argument could be made.

The sheriff got down off his horse and tried yelling Vaughn's name, but the old man still would not move nor cease his muttered nonsense. After a while it must have been too much for the boy Macon Trent to have to hear that noise and know Vaughn's tongue was as unstrung from known language as his mind from the known world. That must have been why he went to his horse and jerked out his carbine and trained its muzzle on the old man's temple, yelling that he needed to shut his goddamn gob. Painter batted the rifle away and told the boy to stop being a born fool, even though there was no conviction in his voice when he said it.

Painter bent down and scattered leaves under his spread fingers. "How long you known this son-of-a-bitch?"

"Going on thirty years. Used to share a tobacco barn up above Little Big Watch Creek. Hunted with him more times than I can count."

"Anything to suggest something like this?"

Sloane listened to Vaughn's running gibberish, loose and musical and seductive on the stone-deaf air. "Naw, there ain't nothing to suggest something like this."

The judge's son came back in half an hour. He said he needed some hatchets and a bundle of canvas. The Price brothers wanted to know if he and Hiram had found the girl. They had, but it would be a while bringing her back. No one asked why. The judge's son didn't volunteer a thing himself. When he had the tools he'd come for, he rode back out, not asking the others for help.

They took turns sitting with Vaughn. None wanted to be near him for long, Sloane least of all. He took up his cane from the Price boy's equipage and hobbled off to the head of a deep ravine, looking for a place to settle his thoughts. As much as he tried, he couldn't keep his mind off what Hiram and the judge's son must be looking on at that moment. That poor butchered girl. What was it that allowed men to see such things and to carry on?

Sloane knew two great losses in his life, Kite and Nara. And he'd looked on their dead bodies, known the shape of sorrow like a north wind blown clean through him. He understood the price of that kind of suffering. The boy dead by his hand, Nara by her own. But that was what a man with the weight of sin on his back had to feel. He didn't expect God to be tender with him. That's why he'd never believed in the same God Nara worshiped. He didn't want the ease of forgiveness just because he asked for it. Sloane believed in the misery of his own weaknesses. The Lord surely knew he had plenty of them. But why would God show Hiram the things he had? Why punish the undeserving? And why was there no way Sloane could make his son understand how sorry he was? For all of it. All of it so shameful that it clotted his mouth with hopeless silence and knowing he could never make amends.

By the time Sloane came back to the others, the afternoon had grown somewhat cooler and a light mist began to fall through the naked branches. Someone had thrown a blanket over Vaughn, more likely to hide his appearance than to provide him with any comfort from the elements. When it got near dark and Hiram and the judge's son hadn't gotten back, the sheriff reluctantly made preparations for camp. He sent the Price boys out to gather firewood. He asked Sloane to break out the cookware. Though the old man obliged, Sloane doubted anyone would be able to sit down to a plate. He knew the last thing on his mind was his appetite.

They built a big fire, greedy in its need to burn large stacks of wood. The flames scaled and cavorted and drew out just enough light that the men were cut off from anything but the immediate circle of one another's company. The shadows surrounding them were a mercy. With the night blotting out the dead woods, Sloane could almost imagine he was in another place entire. The dark could sometimes be kind that way.

The sheriff heated the same bean paste they'd breakfasted on that morning and served out the bowls. They took them and worked the wooden spoons into the food without passion. Sloane let his bowl sit on the ground and drank his whiskey, not offering to share. He did not mark whether the others noticed this slight or not. Nor did he care. Vaughn kept whispering.

Hiram and the judge's son came into the edge of camp very late and dismounted in the dark. Those in camp could hear that one of them dragged something behind his horse, but it was impossible to say what it was since the two riders remained beyond the firelight. Without saying a word, the judge's son came up out of the night, went over to Vaughn and struck him so hard that he was knocked from his stump to the ground.

The sheriff protested weakly. "That man's a lawful prisoner."

Hiram stepped forward. "Somebody get me some rope."

Trent Price went to his horse and came back with a neat bight strung between upturned palms. The sheriff nervously looked on.

"Now, I won't have you killing that man."

Hiram bent and pried Vaughn's jaw and wrapped the cord three times between his teeth and made it fast where the old man couldn't speak. He then cut the rope with a clasp knife and bound him by his ankles and then lastly his hands. After the prisoner was thus secured, Hiram dragged him a few feet closer to the fire and then reclothed him in the filthy blanket. He took his father's whiskey without asking and drank a full gulp and passed it to the judge's son who did the same.

The judge's son dragged his sleeve across his mouth. "I've got some more in my saddlebags."

"Get it."

After silently watching them drink for a good long while, Macon Price asked what it was they'd all heard being dragged behind the horse.

Spenser's eyes did not meet the boy when he spoke. "Take a look for yourself if you want to."

Price stood and studied the wall of darkness.

Sloane put his hand out. "You don't want to look, son. You know what it is. Clapping eyes on it don't make it no more real."

Hiram lit a cigarette. "I imagine it's none of your goddamn business what he wants. Go ahead, boy. Satisfy your curiosity. Why don't you see what there is left of her?"

Price hesitated, the quivering shadow line of the firelight and the dark beyond moving silently across the rim of human sight. When he stepped out, he went out alone among where the horse stood still limbered to its freight. The others all turned their heads and listened.

When the boy had been out there a very long time, Hiram got up and followed. Sloane heard him tell Price to go back to the fire. The boy's boots scuffed across the dirt and he collapsed without speaking. His eyes seemed to be as dark and clouded as a new bruise.

They could hear Hiram making lashings slack and then the careful settling of a weight on the ground. Sheriff Painter rose to his feet, alarmed.

The judge's son placed his hand on the sheriff's shoulder. "He's letting the horse rest. No creature on this earth deserves to be drawn up all night with the dead."

An hour of drinking passed without words before the men began to unfurl their sleeping rolls on the ground. Even Vaughn allowed his body to slump over as close to the fire as he could without burning himself.

As he walked past, Trent Price kicked coals at the prisoner's head. One nugget lodged in Vaughn's eye socket and the old man began to buck and moan in a moment of startled pain. Sloane leaned forward, pinched the cinder between his fingers and flung it into the dark. Once he was sure there was no more fire caught up in the old man's beard and hair, he poured water from a canteen to soothe the irritation on his fingerprints and then did the same for Vaughn's burns.

Hiram said he'd sleep out there with the girl to keep the animals away. No one offered to bring her into camp.

Whether anyone slept, Sloane couldn't be sure. But they did wrap themselves in their blankets and remained still for a very long time. He closed his eyes and tried to will himself over the quiet edge of oblivion, but the horizon kept sliding on, passing into a black expanse as immense as that very night. The emptiness grew inside his head until he felt like he was alone in an enormous room. He sat up.

The fire still burned, but it had fallen down into a heap on its gradual way to ruin. Sloane shifted one of the logs and sparks danced off and were lost in the dark beyond. He watched them go, mentally mapping their brief constellations. He knew these lesser stars compassed his true sense of direction no better than the ancient ones overhead, but that made them no less lovely in their going. And so he went out there in the place they had vanished, seeking the point where their faintest light was put out by the bluing.

He could hear Hiram sleeping. The heavy exhalation and the pause. The moment when breath reincarnated. Those were the simple seasons of a man's body at rest. The life in him, in his son, a pattern of suffering and recovery, going on and on because the body had no choice but to survive. Not like a mind or heart. Those were the parts that could be so weak, so willing to cede their existence. The mind was an unfenced pasture where the weather and the world could take what it wanted, strip it down to nothing but a patch of hard-tilled earth. But the body was innocent to such easements. The body didn't permit trespass. *Make yourself into the body, son. Make yourself into the body that knows the lasting comfort of its own muscle and bone.*

Nine

They stood in the ashen light of morning looking on the canvas bundle double-wrapped and lashed down against the crossed hickory travois poles. The burial litter of Martha Vaughn. It wasn't much bigger than what would carry a dog.

Trent Price squatted and looked over the humped shape. "Was she that little?"

The judge's son brushed past. "The pieces of her we found was."

Spenser bent and raised the upper end of the poles to the gray horse's haunches so that Hiram could tie each to the saddle's rigging dee. Once he'd tugged the tie points firm to make sure they were good, Hiram stashed his carbine and climbed up and led all of the other horsemen out of the valley.

Sloane was content to never lay eyes on this place again. He rode with the sheriff, glancing back to the rear where the catatonic Vaughn rode at the end of the march with the judge's son. Sloane, for one, was uneasy about having him any closer.

The water crossing was easy. Most of the rains had drained off from the higher elevations and the river ran smooth and uncharged. They saw beavers repairing the storm damage done to old dams and otters poking their sleek heads from banked dens only to draw them quickly back, afraid to seem too optimistic so soon perhaps.

Back on familiar ground, the ride picked up. The old paths were broad and undeviating, and even though Hiram was dragging a sad weight, they did not match their pace to their mood. By noon they'd reached Black's Creek, and then it was only a short way on to Sloane's cabin.

Sloane served what lunch he could from his mostly bare larder. Not much more than some cornbread and old turnips. But at least he was able to set them up with a couple of pints of whiskey, knowing the hooch runner would be back around any day now. Sloane figured he could afford to ration his stores until then. They didn't bother loosening Vaughn's bonds to feed him. The only concession made to the murderer's welfare was a cupful of creek water the judge's son dribbled into the corner of his mouth. They guessed he must have swallowed it because he didn't once choke.

Hiram came up to the cabin. "Well, we better press on."

He'd washed his face down by the creek while the others were eating and his hair was slick and jet. He stood on the edge of the porch, one foot already down to the top step, hat held by the crown, looking as ready to get going on as could be imagined.

Sloane looked off. "You all are welcome to overnight here. Make a strong pull of it to Canon City first thing in the morning."

"Naw, we can make it in by tonight."

Though the others must have known there was no way that was true, none said anything.

"Well, all right then. You can't say that I didn't offer."

"No, I guess you're right about that. Goodbye, Daddy."

"All right, then." Sloane stood on his porch watching them go. When they were out of sight, he went inside the cabin and closed the door on all of that.

His back was flaming up so he tried to rest in bed, but no matter which way he laid the old hurt kept nipping at him. The best he could do was turn to his side so that he faced the little square window painted silver with afternoon light. It was the sight of the leafy trees moving in the wind more than the position that soothed him. A few martins came and went, darting and flapping and squawking. He'd strung a line of gourds out there in the side yard so a colony of them would take up to watch over a little garden patch he'd meant to put in. The little homebody birds had come, but someway or another, that garden had never gotten planted. He liked having them out there all the same. There was something so peaceful about a dependable little family sharing the place with him. Maybe he'd get around to the garden here pretty soon. He still might be able to get some late crops in the ground, something he could can for the winter. He never liked to dismiss a possibility.

He made himself get up at suppertime and built a small fire in the woodstove. He turned up a strip of salt pork from the meat box and cooked it into some bean soup and ate slowly in the dark house, knowing he'd have to make a trip into Lincoln soon. He had never counted on having to feed a posse after all. The jar would need to be sounded to see how much money was left. He might have to ask for credit, but he was sure they'd give it to him. He'd always been good to pay his debts, even after Nara died.

He remembered that last morning she walked out of the cabin with him still pretending to sleep. He even remembered hearing the door ease shut and thinking it was odd she should be up at that time. It was midafternoon before he would find her in the creek, the billow of her skirt as dark as rot. Then, only a week after she'd been buried, the government letter had come and made it worse.

After she was dead he starved himself down, deciding to let nature carry him off. He wanted to let the pain of his empty stomach prepare him, to eat him from the inside out. But something happened, some basic animal within him refused to die and this animal took over his will. He rode down to Lincoln for resupply. When he came into town, he was so famished he couldn't simply buy the food he needed to carry back. He rode right up to the front of the Rabbit Hole Hotel, strode directly into the dining room, and ordered a plate of fried chicken and collard greens and corn bread. He ate that plate and doubled his order and cleaned that one as well. He ate like he was trying to split himself wide open to the world.

One of the fellow diners who happened to be there that day was the resident postmaster. He finished his own portions of the evening's fare and came over to Sloane. He had not heard of Nara's death so he didn't offer condolences. Instead, he thought to let Sloane know that another certified letter bearing a government return address had arrived in his office just that very morning, much like the one from a few weeks earlier, and he'd be happy to unlock the office so that he could give it to him. Sloane was confused to hear that the postmaster referred to "another" letter since he knew of none.

Sloane paid his bill and followed the postmaster across the packed dirt road to the little whitewashed clapboard post office. He signed a chit acknowledging his receipt, thanked the postmaster for his kindness and stepped back outside. On his way over to the store to purchase provisions, he stuffed the letter into his front shirt pocket. He knew the letter held something important, but he needed to be back home before he dared open it. On the ride back, he could feel the outline of the envelope burning through his shirt, through his old skin, fusing to the hot cinder inside his chest. That was what it was like to carry that still unread message, to bear it back to a place that was not just an empty cabin, but a home full of graves.

With all the stores put away, he sat at the rough-hewn kitchen table looking at the letter for a long time; a coal-oil lamp hung from the joist overhead. The night came on full and the darkness without was so complete that the cone of lamplight did little to dispel the shadows grown large on the floor and walls. He cut the paper seam with his penknife and read the odd hieroglyph of typewritten words.

```
15 August 1918

From: Department of the Navy Division of
Noti cation and Records, Washington, D.C.
To: The Family of Corporal Hiram Tobit, United
States Marine Corps

Dear Mr. and Mrs. Tobit:

It is with great pleasure we would like to
inform you that the letter sent on 23 July
1918 informing you of your son's wounding and
```

subsequent mortality in Belleau Wood, France,
was the result of a grievous administrative
error. A confusion in service numbers caused
a false notification of death. At the time of
this letter, your son remains on active duty
proudly serving his country and the United
States Marine Corps. We are assured he is
a credit to his unit in the ongoing campaign against European aggressors. Please accept the personal thanks sent on behalf of
the Commandant of the Marine Corps and the
President of the United States of America.

(signed)
2nd Lieutenant Franklin Pearce
Division of Notification and Records, Annex G

He read the letter three times; each time slower than the last. Comprehension took root and forked deep down. Numbness became overall and complete. He folded the letter and returned it to its envelope and sat there without sleeping for the rest of the night.

When dawn broke he went into his bedroom and opened the chifforobe. He hadn't touched any of Nara's things since she'd died, fearing the scent of her would overthrow him. But with purpose set firmly in his mind, her powders and dainties didn't bear symbol nor suggestion of her. They were simply obstacles, paraphernalia of some greater secret that he needed to uncover, to prove to himself a reason lay behind her suicide.

The letterbox lay near the bottom beneath a small stack of handkerchiefs. He opened it and saw inside a string-bound bundle of handwritten letters. He recognized Hiram's handwriting. The other letter, however, the one with the oddly lovely typing, lay separately at the bottom. He read it, reading the past more than the message itself.

Standing beside Nara when she held it. Reading the lapsing time, the way the news of Hiram's death must have attached itself to everything she saw and heard. Time drawn thin and raw and peeling away so fine it was just a perforated and transparent skin.

And then the second letter, the one that arrived too late. The one the postmaster had so kindly retrieved for him. What was that—a simple error? Was that what had killed her, accident? Men called things they didn't understand accidents, but that didn't make them any less real as instruments of fate. Just as Sloane himself had been an instrument of fate when he mistook the shape in the bushes for a coyote instead of his oldest boy and pulled the trigger. At least there was some consolation in knowing such events were fixed in God's mind, decided. Just because a thing didn't at first seem to belong to God, didn't mean it wasn't so.

That's how he'd lived with it for the past two years. Believing Nara's death was a patch in the same crazy quilt that held together the history of their family. Part of the same fabric of Kite being shot and his own drinking and Hiram going off to war. Every bit of their sorrow and loss bound by the invisible threads of God's plan.

But when Hiram came back home in his marine uniform, Sloane began to have doubts. There was something in the boy that called up the lost years. He had been able to let her rest, satisfied that his love for his wife was such that he didn't want to wish her a ghost in his heart. But when Hiram came back, it was as though something was breathed back into him, filling him with the hurt he'd though buried. A want had grown in him to find Nara and bring her up out of the earth, to set her properly so that there could be no way her bones and soul were at odds with what God wished.

Her burying had been a convenience for Sloane. He'd not wanted to know exactly where that no-good Sluder boy had dug the hole and taken her, because it would have been too hard knowing exactly where the closed place in the earth was. The permanence of her being gone would have done worse than kill him. He knew what it was like to bury a loved one. That was the mistake he'd made with Kite. There wasn't a single time in the years since that he'd walked past that spot of ground and not remembered the bitterness of pointless sacrifice. But he could take that burden. He would be a hypocrite not to. It was that he hadn't been strong enough to double that weight. He'd told Sluder to pick the gravesite himself and be done with it. Then he had gone inside and stepped back to his empty bedroom to crawl into bed, lying next to the impressed silhouette in the sheets where he'd laid her body out. He could hear digging, but that was all.

Now the fire in the cookstove had died down and his bean soup had become cold and clotted. He eased up from the chair and hobbled over to where his cane leaned against shelves of old crockery and stumped out to the front porch where the moon was a guillotined head above the mountains. Though it would still be summertime for a good two months, there was that bite of refreshing evening cool that could send a body off to sleep quick. But he was not tired, wouldn't be for some hours.

Sometimes Sloane felt so old he believed only the mountains could understand him. Perhaps that was why he never took much stock in words. He was a hand at telling stories, true enough, but that was just tongue wagging, the easy pace of talking without having to concern himself with the saying of it. With all the campfires he'd sit around, there hadn't been any learning to speak of, just listening to all the old folks talking up a storm and then putting his own voice to the tales. With Hiram it was different. He used the sharp angles of language like it was something that could cut. The boy had been that way ever since his mother first sent him to that schoolteacher all those years ago.

Hiram learned many things from that schoolteacher very quickly. But what he learned first and best was how to goad his father. Whenever he was alone with Sloane, Hiram would talk on and on about his books and equations. Even his reading of the old Bible stories changed under his tutor. Hiram said those sacred stories weren't real to him anymore but merely signs open to each man's interpretation. Then he'd act like he should be patted on his back for his common blasphemy.

Sloane had never abided another man lording a single thing over him. He knew he was prideful and should guard against a sin that lay so heavy on his heart, but each time Hiram preached against the ignorance of the world, it was like another stick of wood was being added to the fire secretly burning inside Sloane. Because though Hiram might say the word "world" Sloane knew that he meant the word "father." And wasn't that a kind of blasphemy too?

Sloane knew he had been a good son himself. Always obedient and cheerful to his father's wishes and directions, he felt lucky to have been sired by a living hero. This feeling was so strong that even as an old man he trembled before the idea of his long-dead father, not because he had been a hard or fearsome man, but because that was the proper law of fathers and sons. Even now, Sloane repeated the old family stories as a way to honor him. He felt that it was his duty as the son of a great man.

Then there had been that day when all the stoked resentment ran to full flame. Sloane had finally been spared the schoolteacher and for months Hiram's lectures tapered off. Because Sloane was looking for any signs of a quelled rebellion under his own roof, he mistook his son's reticence for peace. But then the boy mentioned college. Spoke of it as if it were a mere convenience. That was what ignited Sloane's rage. The easiness with which Hiram cast things. As if it were a simple matter of only deciding he should have a thing and wait for fate to immediately bend to his whim. As if every man didn't have such dreams for himself.

Sloane did not realize he'd slapped his son until he felt the pain in his hand afterwards. He sensed the curve of his boy's face pressed into a bright, ringing red against his palm. Oddly, this was what concerned him most. Not his child's body lying on the floor, but the fleeting fear that the real Hiram was caught up in his hand's crevices. For a moment, Sloane was careful not to spread his fingers and palm too wide lest his soul slip from his grasp and tumble shapelessly into the dark.

From that greater dark to the lesser one where he now sat remembering, Sloane had learned to regret much since that day he struck his only living son. That was wisdom for old men. That was the pain that paid the debt of a whole country of sleepless nights. Thinking on this, he braced his back and stood and went quietly into his cabin, the rollicking night birds singing him no angry songs as he went.

Ten

The whiskey runner rode right up to the front of the house on a sorrel, kicked one long leg over with the other, and slid from his saddle straight to the ground in a single practiced motion. As soon as his moccasins lit on the grass, he swung his hat from his bald head and flashed a sunlit smile as wide as greed itself. Sloane had watched him coming from as far as the creek ford. In that time he'd made a good long study of him and figured the peddler for being a mite too enthusiastic to be believed.

The whiskey runner shook his head like he was trying to shed himself of that smile but just couldn't. "If it ain't my best customer."

"I figured you'd written me off as dead."

"No, sir, I'll tell you the truth of it, Mr. Tobit. I just plumb forgot to make my way up here. Regular business has been right slow of late, so I turned my hand at some odd jobs for a bit."

Sloane didn't know how much of the lie to believe or

whether he should even care. He tipped his head toward the horse. "What'd you bring?"

The wicked smile slackened at its corners. "Well, sir, I've brought some peach brandy and some mighty fine corn liquor if you'd care for a smidge."

Sloane didn't need to say a word. That he was still standing there conveyed his interest. The hooch runner loped backed to his horse and brought out two pint jars, one clear the other the color of new honey. "You got a preference?"

"I prefer both."

The hooch runner laughed. Sloane knew he must already be calculating costs in his head.

They sat at the kitchen table with the door opened to let in a breeze. It was another hot and cloudless day and the sun was a malevolence over everything. Sweat slid down the back of Sloane's neck and paused there at the uppermost ledge of his spinal column, waiting for some further misery before it coursed down the full length of his body. Two mugs, dirty and empty, were set on the otherwise cleared table between the two men. The hooch runner placed each of the jars near the mugs and gently pried off the lids with a sweet-sounding pop. Even Sloane's old nose could smell the harsh air rising.

The hooch runner poured two half mugs of the corn liquor. "I hope you don't mind if I join you."

"Help yourself."

They drank and sucked at their teeth.

"Not too bad, is it?"

"It'll get the job done."

After they'd drunk the mugs down to the bottom, Sloane's head was unpleasantly light in the heat. He stood up and drew a cupful of spring water from the pump. The hooch runner refilled his own mug with a dram of the brandy and sipped it lightly. "To be honest, it was the goings-on in town that remembered you to me."

"What goings-on you talking about?"

"That business with the man who cut up his girl. I saw that son of yours riding in with him and the sheriff and I got to asking and found out you'd been up there to help find him, bring the son-of-a-bitch to justice."

Sloane swallowed half of the water and then rinsed his mouth and spat back into the sink. "Just told them where the old deer camp was, is all."

"Boy, I tell you. That is something I never thought I'd see around these parts."

"No, I reckon we all could go without seeing something like that. How much do I owe you for that there moonshine?"

"Two dollars. I figure that pays for my time and labor."

Sloane shook his head and watched the grass standing still in the windless yard. "That's mighty high for two little ole bottles of homebrew."

"Two dollars apiece, I mean." The whiskey man hid his face in the mug.

Sloane reached into the coffee tin and held the money in his hands, fanning the fine paper edges across the pad of his thumb. This was time he was holding, time he'd put into dragging crops out of the earth. Time saved back. To be spent now on what? He handed it over.

"What else you got to barter? This ain't enough."

Sloane led him through the cabin, letting him look through his few possessions. The hooch runner's eyes lit on nothing save for a pair of large oval mirrors with silver frames. They'd been hung side by side in the bedroom to catch the window light and project it throughout the otherwise dark room.

"How bout them?"

"Two more pints."

The hooch runner ran his fingers over black chin stubble. "I reckon we can arrange that."

Sloane took the mirrors down and handed each over, careful to keep the glass facing out so that he didn't catch any piece of his own reflection. The hooch runner hefted them under each arm and walked them on out to his horse. He rigged them carefully facing outward with lashings run through the tops of the frames so that when they were made fast they hung at an uptilt against the horse's flanks, looking like medallions that had drawn down small portions of the sky above. Once he was sure the mirrors were set as securely as possible, he made good on his promise to deliver the two additional pints of spirits, setting them on the edge of the porch.

Sloane looked at the whiskey. "We're even then."

"Yes, sir, I figure we are." The hooch runner turned to go.

Sloane said, "I been meaning to ask you."

"That right?"

"About that Sluder boy, that one what used to ride with you some. The one what dug that grave for me."

"What about him?"

"I just need to ask him something is all. Wondering if you was seeing him anytime soon."

The hooch runner propped one foot back on the porch steps and leaned on his forward leg, thinking. "Well, he does something for me ever now and then, but I wouldn't call him regular help if you know what I mean. What is it you need doing? I'm sure we can come to some sort of arrangement."

"I just need to ask him something is all. I guess he's still down in Canon City then?" Too much to ask that. Now there'd be no way to get anything out of the hooch runner. Not once he knew he had some information that could be of value.

The hooch runner dragged his foot from the porch and stood looking off at the trees. There wasn't a thing out there for him to see. "There's no telling where a fool like that keeps his body."

Sloane spat. "All right. I guess you'd better take it easy with them mirrors. Don't want to lay a crack in them."

"Naw, there ain't no danger of that."

The hooch runner went on and climbed into the saddle and turned the sorrel back out towards Black's Creek, the mirrors sliding up and down against the horse's rounded haunch, the reflections of the light and tree line playing across the quicksilver surface. Even once the horse was lost from sight behind the lush understory of trees and vines, Sloane could see glinting stripes of sun scooting out in random quaking patterns on the grass before him, the mere figment of light projected even this far. He stood there watching the weird geometric ballet until not a single ray could be seen and then he sat down and began to drink the peach brandy straight from the jar.

He drank through the quick flush of nausea until he could feel nothing more than a warmth inside that chased away the discomfort of the humid afternoon. Still he sweat, but all of the concerns of the body were at a distance now and he was free to think without the pained nearness of his weakened joints and muscles. That was the purity in the drinking and it was as clean and strong as any fire.

When finally he stood after drinking a good half pint, he no longer needed his cane. He still felt the loom of pain, but it lay out behind him like his own afternoon shadow. He knew it was there, but its presence had grown irrelevant. Another lie he allowed himself to believe, but a vital one if he was going to do what he had in mind.

He headed out to the tool shed, opened the door and braced his hand to the jamb. The darkness inside was more than he'd counted on and he had to stare it down for a full minute before he could see the objects within. Even when he could, the tools were a mess of snapped handles and dislodged heads so that trying to find what he was looking for was like trying to put together a puzzle of incongruent pieces. After a while, he saw one of the spades leaning business end up in one of the back corners. He rolled the door back as far as he could with his shoulder, knowing it would begin to swing shut as soon as he let go. He hurried to the back. He almost had his hands to it when the hinges moaned and the shrinking triangle of light on the floor crushed itself down thin as a chalk line. Once more, he was blind.

"Well, goddammit."

He swept his hands out, knocking over a pair of posthole diggers with a loud and iron-weighted clatter. As a result, something else was tipped, and a chain of invisible crashing rained down around his feet, thumping and clanging anonymously. He swore and kicked at the mess, incurring bruises he wouldn't feel for another several hours, but the action took his breath and appeased his rising anger enough to give him a chance to rethink his efforts. Carefully, he extended his fingers until he could feel the coarse edge of the back wall. As if by spell, the handle slipped into his palm and he knew by touch he had the tool he needed.

The sun was a dizzy curve when he stepped outside, but he didn't let that deter him. He paced off the distance from the porch to the general area where he remembered hearing the Sluder boy dig a place for Nara. He felt as though something was attracting him, his internal sense of direction drawn out as neat as if it were a compass needle.

When he'd gone far enough he sunk the shovel tip. The moist ground suctioned to the scooped iron and broke free as he lifted the spade, a quiet plop in the grass when he turned the handle. Cut worms dangled and probed their split selves to a sun-blind world. A mole's corridor collapsed on itself and then was erased by the ongoing excavation. Sloane kept digging.

He was a foot down when he began to rethink his positioning. There was no way, he reasoned, he could be sure so early, but this seemed too far from the house. True, he didn't know the exact distance, but he was turning old roots and stones that should have been dislodged when the Sluder boy buried her. He paused and listened to the answering quiet.

True silence. This is the language God speaks.

By suppertime he was down three feet and the obstructions only grew larger and more permanent in their appearance. He flung the shovel out and climbed up with difficulty. His head hurt and the ache in his back was no longer the vague afterthought it had been early in the day.

Despite the work, Sloane wasn't hungry. Instead, he dragged one of the chairs out on the porch and drank the rest of the brandy while he studied the pointless hole in the ground. He knew he might never find her like this, following the memory of sounds he'd only partially heard.

He knew then there was no other way. He had to find the Sluder boy and bring him back up to have him point out the spot. He would remember. He had to.

He woke in the chair sometime in the middle of the night, still drunk. He tried to stand, but his legs were on soft ground and so he soon gave up. It was better to be awake through the deepest part of the night. Safe from the nightmares. He turned his head and listened for screech owls and whippoorwills. Always, there was something out on the move, living an invisible life. He sometimes thought that might be a better way for him to exist, awake while the rest of the world slept.

Through the long night watch, his head began to clear, but still he didn't move from the chair. Instead, he waited for the paling of morning. When it came in burnished hues and the birdsong swelled and the wind breathed its lustless breath, Sloane eased from the chair and crossed the yard to the stall where the mule still slept. He spoke nonsense to the animal. He didn't know why. There was some satisfaction in believing the creature comprehended the affection he felt for it. It may have been just an ornery lump of flesh, as oblivious to its fate as a plowshare. But talking to it and feeling its coarse hide beneath his hand made Sloane doubt so.

Since he had no provisions to pack besides the contraband liquor and his cane, he left within only a few minutes, letting the mule walk a slow pace down through the yard and out to the creek ford.

They had made only a couple of miles before Sloane had to stop and rest. He watered the mule in a gruely pool of runoff at the base of granite bluffs. Once the animal was comfortable, he limped off to try to walk through the pain and stood at a slick overlook, his hand braced to the base of his spine. He straightened up as well as he could and looked on the valley and the range of mountains beyond. A blue haze was drawn out like a childish streak of watercolor brushed over the surface of the earth, as if some hand had striven to soften the sharper edges of the world. He let that soak right in to the backs of his eyeballs. When the sight of it pained him more than the pain in his back, Sloane knew it was time to move on. He went back to the mule and resolved not to remember the beauty of such a thing.

Eleven

It took Sloane two days and nights to find the Sluder boy. In that time, he slept where he dropped and ate what he could beg. His liquor was gone by the end of the first day and that made it worse, but he damned the shakes and the cold fever and peered through the visions he knew were invisible to all but him. When he did finally spy the boy it was just after suppertime outside McCrorey's feed store where a card game was running in the backroom. He could hear the hoots and hollers within, but his eyes never left the boy's slouched form pacing back and forth with no definable point of origin or arrival, just a kind of inborn ambling.

"Hey you, Sluder."

The boy stopped and regarded the gloom. The cigarette smoke curled up to the brim of his felt hat, concealing his face. The boy's answer was shaped by an unkind grin. "Hey you, Tobit."

Sloane came forward, tugging the protesting mule by its bridle. "What in the hell you doing with that thing? It smells something awful."

Sloane ignored the question. It was clear the boy didn't welcome his company. Sluder kept turning his head over his shoulder, looking up and down the length of the narrow dirt alley, either waiting for someone or anxious to keep someone away.

"I've been meaning to ask you about something."

"I guess there ain't a way that asking can wait 'til later now, is there?"

Sloane looked at the yellow square of lighted window over the boy's shoulder. He could see only the back of a man's head thick with tousled silver hair. "That work you done for me, couple of years back."

"Burying your woman?"

Sloane swallowed once and nodded. "You remember where exactly it was that you done that? Reckon you might be able to show me?"

Sluder spat the cigarette from his mouth, its embered tip a brief spark in the lowering dark. "Unless I'm dreaming things, my remembering gear has you telling me you didn't ever want to know where I dug it."

"Yeah, that's what I said."

Even though the smoke had cleared away, the dark had come on full and Sloane couldn't see what might have been behind Sluder's eyes. Just then, a short rap sounded from the window, drawing both men's attention. Without explanation, Sluder stepped back and answered the signal by three quick strikes of his palm against the outer window frame. The voices inside swelled once more. Sluder strolled back. "I don't know what to tell you. You can see I'm working."

"Funny business you've gotten yourself in from the looks of it."

"Ain't your concern to look in on my business, Tobit."

The boy's voice had gone hard and his fists now stuck to the points of his hips, elbows jutting. Sloane looked off into the shadow-tenanted night. "I'm willing to pay you for your time."

The boy smirked. "How you figure on doing that? A born blind man can call you for a pauper."

Sloane didn't realize he'd knocked the boy flat with the sweep of his cane until he was already on him, gripping the lapels of his broadcloth jacket like they were the handles of outrage itself. The boy was strong and despite the shock his eyes were still open and fierce and he was trying to wrest himself free by raising up in a wrestler's bridge. Sloane lowered his weight on the boy's chest and butted the crown of his head into Sluder's chin. A thin ribbon of blood spurted from between the boy's teeth. Sloane briefly wondered if Sluder had champed his tongue in two.

The boy kicked out and bucked, trying to strike at Sloane's groin. Sloane clamped his legs tight to fend away Sluder's feet and leveled his cane across the boy's Adam's apple as if he meant to draw a plumb line straight across his throat. With only the slightest exertion of pressure, the boy couldn't breathe.

Sloane had wanted to say something once he had him pinned there, to ask him to help him now that Sluder had no choice but to agree. Sloane knew he would sacrifice nearly anything to escape the simple prison of this boy's idly exercised power over him. But something deep within him refused all human speech. He felt the spasms of the boy fighting wildly, his continued strength a kind of blood insult. The grip of Sluder's fingers bit deep into his weak old man's flesh. The boy looked up, eyes hot with arrogance. Then he did something that made no sense at all. He smiled.

Sloane saw the faintest blur of the cudgel before it struck him full across the temple. The night ruptured stark and pink in a thousand gashes.

Hiram's fingers laced through the jail cell's whitewashed bars. "I wouldn't have figured you for a brawler."

Sloane rose up slow from the bed ticking. There was no frame to elevate him, just a filthy patch of cloth and stitching between him and the concrete floor. For lighting, he had but a single lantern with a cracked red globe like the ones he'd seen railroad men carry. The dimness was not unwelcome though. He could see Hiram was dressed in a new suit. "You headed to church in that pretty outfit?"

"You always this smart when they drag you into the drunk tank?"

Sloane drew up his legs in front of him. "I ain't drunk." He gently felt the marble-sized knot on the side of his head and winced. He looked around and saw his cane was missing. "I can't walk nowhere without my stick."

"I guess they figured you were armed and dangerous."

"I guess they did. You come to gloat or you gonna get me outta here?"

"They got to pull together some paperwork is all. Sit tight, Daddy."

Within a few minutes, Sheriff Painter came over and smiled ruefully as he opened the cell and brought over Sloane's cane. "Mighty sorry about this business, Mr. Tobit. But afraid we didn't have much choice with those other fellers testifying to what you done."

"Sure. I can imagine a group of folks has more say than one all on his lonesome."

"Come on, Daddy. Thank you, Sheriff."

They went outside into the cool evening. Sloane breathed it in deep, just now realizing how stale the jail air had been.

"Well, seeing as how you interrupted my supper, I guess you wouldn't be opposed to sitting down to a meal with me, would you?"

Sloane felt his stomach seize at the suggestion of food. "No, I wouldn't fault you for it at all."

The hotel had mostly cleared and what few patrons remained were drinking coffee, but the man who met them at the entrance to the dining room appeared to know Hiram. They were seated and given a pair of paper menus. Sloane squinted at the writing and then shoved it across the linen tablecloth.

"Order me whatever you're getting. I don't want to be called particular."

"I'd hardly dream of it."

When the roasted beef and potatoes came it was on large plates and it was so hot they had to let it sit for a while before they could eat. Sloane gnawed on a dinner roll dabbed in gravy and studied the lavish red drapes sashed and bowed like parade-ground bunting.

"You living fancy for a army recruiter, ain't you?"

Hiram picked up his fork and knife and began carving a medallion of beef. "Call it a special occasion."

Sloane looked at the array of silverware laid down on either side of his plate. He made a best guess and went to it. "I never meant to inconvenience you. I had business with that boy."

"Seems to me he and his friends didn't care for your idea of business."

"No, I guess not."

The waiter brought two tall glasses of water. Sloane could see the waiter's eyes wrinkling at the corners, as if the man had caught wind of something foul.

"They don't serve no whiskey here?"

Hiram nodded his thanks to the waiter. "Prohibition law. They'd be shut down if they did."

Sloane sniffed. "Mountains sure are changing."

"Yes, sir. I suppose that's true. Anyhow, it's just as well you came along when you did."

"That right?"

"The lawyers will be wanting you as a witness."

"Witness to what?"

"What we saw up there when we brought Matt Vaughn back. I tried to keep it from being discussed so as to keep you clear, but those Price boys are bad to gossip. Everybody and God knows who was in on the posse. They'll be no keeping you from it. The sheriff's already sent along for the circuit judge since old Judge Spenser decided to retire himself. Too smart to get caught up in a mess like this, I imagine."

Sloane stared down at the slices of gristly meat. "I'm not much for answering some lawyer's questions."

"Be that as it may, they're gonna ask just the same. You can bunk with me over at the boarding house."

"I don't want to put you out."

"There's a cot the widow will loan me. It shouldn't be more than a couple of weeks at the most. I already took your mule over to the house stall. There's a little boy over there that will look to it as good as he does my horse."

Sloane stilled his shaking hand before he reached it across the table to drink from his water glass. "Well, son, if that's the case, I guess there's not much more this body can do."

Hiram made Sloane comfortable in the bed and told him the house rules. He even fetched up a jar of shine from downstairs and placed it atop a chest of drawers, saying to resort to it only in case of emergency. Sloane could tell his son understood the thing inside he was fighting. That meant something. Once Sloane was all settled for the night, Hiram placed his fancy hat on his head and started to leave.

"What about that cot you was speaking so highly of?"

Hiram's face flushed in the dark. "I still got places to go this evening."

"Those places got cots of their own to sleep in, I'll bet."

"Good night, Daddy."

He listened to Hiram's light footfalls fade along the hallway and down the staircase. The gentle sound seemed to add dimension to the strange house. Sloane hadn't slept in any place other than his own in so many years. The hollowed-out bigness frightened him a little. It was nothing at all like his cabin. It struck him as odd that Hiram could so easily shift himself from place to place. Always ready to pick up and move on. He wondered what that did to a man over a period of time. What did home mean to someone who was always stretching the ends of the Earth to find a place to sit and rest? What did it mean about all the places he'd left behind?

The town was quiet and dark but Sloane's thoughts railed. He could feel the old shivers coming on him and he turned his head to the wall so that he wouldn't have to look at the jar of liquor across the room. But the more he concentrated on not laying his eyes on the object, the more definite the image became in his mind. He saw the way the moonlight lacquered it with shades of silver and blue, as clean and honed as an oiled razorblade.

He swung himself up and sat on the edge of the bed. He saw the jar, a cool, pale globe suspended in the dark. He wondered why he even bothered fighting it. What was he trying to prove? He'd come too far in his years to change who he was now. But still, something kept him rooted where he was. Something kept him sober. Maybe for once there was cause to listen to whatever that something was.

Twelve

The boy Albert showed Sloane where the recruiting office was and walked along the whole way to keep him company. He seemed like a kind little boy, respectful and quiet. It pleased Sloane to be around Albert. In the few days since he'd been in the boarding house both the boy and the widow had gone out of their way to make him feel welcome. He even suspected the widow woman had set her cap in his direction. She wasn't bad looking, just a bit distracted by her own brooding. The last thing in the world he needed, though, was a sour woman.

Sloane poked his head through the door and rattled his cane against the doorframe. Hiram looked up from a sheaf of papers. "Afternoon, Daddy. Grab a seat. We'll be heading along here in a few minutes."

Sloane waved goodbye to Albert through the front window and hobbled inside the office. While he sat there waiting, he studied the different posters hung on the wall behind the desk. Each of the pictures showed young men wearing the same uniform Hiram did, but the artist had drawn great smiles on their tomato-red faces. The posters made it look like charging a machine gun nest was the most joyful thing a young man might decide to do. "Boy, they make it look pretty, don't they?"

Hiram glanced up and saw where his daddy was looking. "Pictures don't make much of a difference what boys decide to do."

"I'm just saying. What does?"

"What does what?"

"Make a difference."

Hiram stopped writing and laid his pencil aside. "Why, you figure on enlisting?"

"Just curious, is all. You don't have to be hateful about it."

"Let me get this done, will you? Then we can get on."

"I ain't keeping you from nothing."

Sloane ventured not a word for several minutes. When Hiram finished with his papers, he plucked his hat from the nail on the wall and they both stood without a word and went on out the front. The sun was full and sharp and cut precise shadows on the dirt. They trampled their own silhouettes underfoot as they walked across the square to the courthouse.

Sheriff Painter greeted them at the top of the stone steps and wrung their hands. He was dressed in a good but heavy suit. His face was the color of tender beef and sweat darkened his shirt collar. He wore a baleful smile. "Mr. Tobit, you'll be glad to know I've talked to that Sluder boy about the fracas."

"That right?"

"Yes, sir. He says he understands it was likely a misunderstanding, it being late in the evening and all. Anyhow, he's not interested in pursuing anything further against you. He says he's happy to live and let live."

Sloane shuffled forward, placing himself in the cool marble shade of the foyer. He wondered at the sheriff's stupidity. "Well, ain't this just a world fit for small kindnesses."

The sheriff cleared his throat and addressed himself to Hiram. "That lawyer's just down the hall next door to my office. You all should head on down."

Hiram thanked him. He and Sloane walked on.

The lawyer had an assistant, a middle-aged woman with yellow hair balled up at the back of her neck. She told them they were to come in only one at a time in order to ensure their testimonies weren't adulterated. That was her word, not theirs. She wore shoes that made her seem taller than she was and her voice was about as smooth as a cocklebur. Sloane could see she was thinking the word *hillbilly* so strong, it wrapped around her head like a perfume. Hiram went first, leaving Sloane to sit by himself on a long black bench in the hallway. "Don't go running off now."

Sloane said nothing. The door eased shut.

The hall was a rare kind of lonesome. Every step someone took on the floor between offices was a long drop of sound into the bottom of a deep and invisible hole. A large clock hung high up at the top of the wall, just below a long narrow rectangle of window. The little bit of sunlight that shone in laid a silver bar right across the clock face, as if this greater sense of time was wrestling against the man-made symbol. But as the minutes dragged on, the little bar was drawn slightly higher and higher until it retreated up to the cornice and eventually the ceiling. The clock hands kept circling round, steady in their finely milled purpose.

The woman called for him while Hiram was still inside.

He wondered if she had made a mistake or maybe he'd heard her wrong. But when he didn't move, she came out all a-fluster. "They're waiting in there on you, Mister!" It looked like it was all she could do to keep from spitting fire when she talked.

"All right, then. I guess I'll be along shortly."

When he came into the office, Hiram and the lawyer were shaking hands and talking.

"Ah, Mr. Tobit. Please, go ahead and take a seat. Your son and I were just remembering a place in France, a little drinking establishment quite popular among the troops during the war." The lawyer was chuckling a little when he said this.

"You and he in the Marines together, then?"

The lawyer faintly blushed. "Well, no, not exactly. I served as a member of the legal corps. A lawyer for soldiers facing court-martial. I wasn't a fighting man like your son here."

Sloane didn't care for the way the lawyer talked. He figured him for a Yankee.

"You'll excuse us, Sergeant?"

"I'll see you back at the house, Daddy. Remember, we got supper plans."

"Sure now."

Sloane sank into one of the leather chairs. It creaked like something alive. The lawyer glanced at some handwritten notes and drew up his own chair a few feet away, leaving only a corner wedge of the mahogany desk between the two of them.

"You must be proud of your son, him being a decorated war hero."

Through the window the mountains loomed over the

lawyer's shoulder, pinchbeck and depthless. "Wouldn't know to speak of it. He keeps to himself on that account."

"I see." Sloane was sure he didn't. "I hope we can get through this fairly quickly. It doesn't appear there's much difference between everyone's stories so far. I've talked both with the sheriff and Judge Spenser's son, and everything has been of a piece. Of course, each set of eyes will see the same thing differently."

Sloane waited.

"There is an interesting difference in your perspective, though. It seems you're the only member of the party who had a prior acquaintance with the man accused."

"Most folks that have been around a place for a time know something of each other."

The lawyer's hair was thin and fine, almost the color of straw. It made his already soft face look even more womanish. Maybe that was the exchange he'd gotten by hiring that woman in the next room for his assistant. Her with the voice and posture of a man to counterbalance this honeyed tongue of his.

"You smoke, Mister Tobit?"

Sloane allowed he was partial to a cigar upon occasion. The lawyer smiled, reached into his pocket, and palmed two cheroots. "I suspected we might find common ground."

The lawyer lit Sloane's cigar first and then his own. Blue smoke flooded the room.

"Did you know Mr. Vaughn's daughter?"

Sloane glanced at the lawyer's notes but couldn't decipher the shorthand. "I'd seen her about over the years. She helped my late wife with church fixings at Easter a few years back. I guess she was just twelve or thirteen at the time."

The lawyer rapidly scribbled. "You never saw Mr. Vaughn lay a hand on her?"

"I can't claim that I did." He remembered the little girl Martha Vaughn had been, all got up in her Easter dress, leaning over the counter beside Nara, both of them working their long fingers into the baking dough, the hair on their forearms powdered and slanting in the motey light.

"You saw what Mr. Vaughn did to her?"

Nara had always coveted a little girl. Whenever her kin came through she'd play the aunt to all the little gals they brought with them, coddling and mewing over them as if they were her own. She could make up a fine doll out of some picked bone and rag, etch a face with a paring knife and paint it up like a store-bought pretty.

"I only saw what my boy and the judge's son brought back. It didn't look like much."

Maybe it would have been easier to have a girl child. She would have been a good hand for staying close to home. Not so anxious and set in her ways. Might even have known how to care better for Nara, eased her through all the loss that lay on her heart heavy as a foundation stone.

"Did Mr. Vaughn say anything while you were sitting with him? Did he confess anything?"

Little Martha Vaughn, sweet as a clear-water creek. He recalled she had a fine singing voice. He'd sat in the church house beside Nara and heard her sing "Onward Christian Soldiers" as if her soul had already flown up to the lip of heaven and got her breath straight out of the sky's ceiling. But that had been years ago. Time had passed. Now she was just a few joints and skin the other side of the ground.

"No, he didn't confess anything," Sloane said. "I couldn't understand a goddamn word he said."

Sloane shaved for the first time in nearly a week. Hiram had bought him a new straight razor and strop at the general store and sent it along to the boarding house with Albert to make sure he was done up proper for evening suppertime. Hiram wanted him to meet this woman he'd been seeing. Sloane didn't know what he was supposed to think of that. His son had never been a fool for women. Always too caught up with his books and dreams to ever allow himself such an earthly concern. Apparently, that was just one more thing the war had changed about him.

Sloane studied his reflection in the mirror. With the whiskers gone, years had fallen from his face. He touched the tips of his fingers to the brightly scrubbed skin. Strange to see how much youth still lingered there, a forgotten twin of the old man he normally was. With the application of the blade and soap a new form appeared. The same thin nose and deep-set eyes as Hiram. The same intent gaze. Nara once said such a look was bad enough to blister. Sloane wondered why such a thing should be passed from father to son.

Hiram entered from the front door and stepped up behind him, his son's face appearing alongside his own in the mirror. The moment matched his thoughts so well, Sloane thought he might be dreaming. But then Hiram spoke and the sound of his voice jarred Sloane back to the here and now. "I bought a suit for you."

Sloane squinted at Hiram in the mirror, a small, white towel haltering his naked shoulders. "I ain't ashamed of my clothes."

Hiram dumped the brown paper package on the bed. Sloane watched him go over to the dresser and eyeball the mason jar of liquor. "Sober as a house mouse. I'll have to say I'm impressed."

Sloane leaned over and splashed little waves of water against the traces of shaving soap clinging to his jowls. He tasted something acrid. "I talked to the widow about this woman you're taking me to meet."

"That a fact?"

Sloane went to the bed and cut through the string bundle with a clasp knife and carefully unfolded the brown paper, revealing a folded coat and trousers, both the color of May blueberries. Hiram handed him a fresh white shirt from the dresser. Sloane unbuttoned the top two buttons before slipping the shirt over his head like a blouse. He went to the mirror and looked at himself again. "I hope you know what you're getting yourself into."

"What's that supposed to mean?"

"This woman. The widow seems to think she ain't just fooling with you."

"Who says I'm just fooling with her?"

"Nobody said nothing. Hand me them britches."

Sloane peeled down his overalls until they were a pool of dust and denim at his feet. He kicked them off along with his unlaced boots. The line of grit at his belly went all the way to the tips of his toes. It was like he'd been sewed around the middle, everything above his navel as clean as a cloud, everything below the color of a slit trench.

"God Almighty, Daddy, I thought I asked you to clean yourself up."

Sloane scowled and went over to the basin and splashed the foul water on his naked thighs, cutting the dust with long muddy sluiceways that ran all over the floor. Hiram snapped the towel from around his father's neck and went to mopping.

Sloane made his way to the bed. "When'd you get so particular?" His back was beginning to act up. He glanced round for his walking stick before he saw it resting in the corner. He allowed himself the ease of the mattress corner and pulled the trousers on. They were loose in the waist, but nothing a short bight of rope wouldn't take care of. Then he remembered the string and cinched it tight around his middle. He stood and tugged at the seams and the waistline remained snug. He brought his arms up level with his shoulders, opening himself to Hiram's visual inspection. "Satisfied?"

"Try the coat."

He did so. It hung from his stooped frame like a cape.

"You'll need some brogans too, I guess."

"I ain't a damn scarecrow."

"Just stand there a minute."

Sloane gazed out the window to the backyard while Hiram rifled through the closet. The clothes itched, but he willed himself to move not a jot.

"Here, try these."

He slipped the shoes onto his feet. They swung loose, but he managed to keep them from flinging off when he took a few steps.

"How's that?"

"They're fine. Just fine."

They took the horse to spare the physical stress of walking, Sloane doubling up in the saddle with his son. It was a cool evening with the first breath of an early autumn in the air. There would be few sweet evenings like this one.

The weather was bad to turn once the leaves changed colors. Best to drink in the peace of a night like this while it was offered.

It didn't take too long to reach the cabin. Hiram went right up to the porch and helped Sloane down before he tied the gray horse to the railing and led him to the door. They waited once he'd banged on the door.

The squirmiest little girl Sloane had ever laid eyes on swung the door open and wrenched herself around in a pirouette when she saw who had come. "It's Sergeant, it's Sergeant!" She took off like she'd been shot with a charge.

Hiram stepped on in and Sloane followed. He saw right away it was as snug a place as any man could desire. There was a big tricolored quilt hung up above a stout fireplace and two big coal-oil lanterns fixed to the wall with brass sconces. Right off to the side was a den with a pair of cushioned rocking chairs and a table bristling with fresh cut daisies. Directly opposite it a small kitchen with a stone wall was filled up with all manner of steaming pots and dishes where the little girl and her lovely momma stirred up a mess of something that smelled delicious.

The pretty dark-haired woman smiled and nodded. "Welcome, Mr. Tobit. We're pleased you've come to visit. Note, honey, why don't you go on and take their coats?"

"Yessum." The little girl popped down from her stool, licking something dark and congealed from her fingers. "Menfolk, I'll be taking your hats and frocks."

They stripped themselves accordingly and gave up the required articles of clothing. The little girl disappeared into one of the backrooms.

Cass called to them. "Both of you rest yourselves. I'll have the table set shortly."

They each took a rocker and sat staring at anything but each other while they quietly waited. It wasn't long before Note relieved them of their awkward silence.

"Rope any more recruits, Sergeant?"

"Not this week. I've been busy with other things."

She nodded wisely. "Oh, I've heard. It's the trial coming up, ain't it?"

Cass slammed an iron spoon into a pan. "Note!"

"It's okay, Momma. Everybody in town knows about the trial of that feller what cut up his daughter. Bad business they all say."

Sloane was upset to hear the girl speak of such. "How'd you hear this talk?"

Note shrugged. "Nobody's keepin' it a secret. Don't surprise me none though. This world is just plumb eat up with mean folks."

Cass had Note join her once more in the kitchen where they laid out the supper on a covered table. She lit two red candles, one at each end of the table, and told Hiram and Sloane to come on while it was still good and hot. Sloane scraped out a chair and was relieved to find there was only one fork and knife set beside his plate. Hiram went to lift the covering off the main dish but was stilled by a look from Cass.

"The blessing please, Note."

Sloane watched Hiram bow his head before he bowed his own.

Once the little girl finished, the platters circled round. Sloane helped himself to the steaming turkey and dumplings and a healthy mound of poke salit. The salt and pepper rained over everything. Cass rose from her place to refill Sloane's half-drained glass of sweet milk. "I'm sure you and

Hiram have enjoyed having a chance to visit these past few days, Mr. Tobit."

Sloane nodded, but did not speak with his mouth full. Hiram finally said something. "The trial starts day after tomorrow."

Cass' hand stilled over the milk pitcher. "So soon?"

"They got hold of the circuit judge quicker than they expected. I guess they just want to get it over with as soon as possible."

Sloane leaned back from his plate. "Pleasures me just fine. I'm anxious to get back to my place and make sure ever'thing is took care of."

Hiram scooped a mess of greens onto his plate. "I'm sure nothing's run off you can't catch."

"Man gets lonesome for familiar surroundings, is all."

After supper they took the evening breeze on the front porch. Note played with her raggedy doll while Hiram and Sloane smoked and Cass sipped a glass of mint tea. The crickets were out and sawing like a million hell-bent fiddlers in the sedge. It wasn't the first time Sloane could remember turning his ear to that old sound, but there was something about the music of that evening to suggest he'd never properly heard it.

"You have a mighty pretty place here, Mrs. Chisholm."

Cass smiled. "My daddy has always believed a patch of dirt is the most pleasing thing a body can enjoy. He'd never say we owned it, even though he's held a proper deed as long as I can remember. He says the earth is something that owns you, not the other way around."

Sloane listened once more to the lowering sounds of the evening, wondering if what he heard was the weight of sunlight sinking into its own wake.

• • •

It was late when Hiram and Sloane made their way back to the boarding house, but the widow had done the kindness of leaving the hall lamp burning. Once it was doused, they crept up the stairs amid the moaning of a house otherwise at rest and made their fumbling way to the bedroom. Neither was tired despite the hour and they agreed to a quiet mug of the still untouched corn liquor atop the chest of drawers. Sloane rested his bones in the bed with the pillows doubled up beneath him. Hiram lit a candle and sank into the cane back.

"You've got yourself a mighty pretty one."

"She's easy enough to look at."

They both turned their heads to listen to a distant yell sounded from somewhere beyond the city square, a jubilant parentheses within the otherwise solemn night.

"They mean to start filling the jury box as soon as the new judge gets to town."

"That right?"

Hiram sucked his gums and nodded. "They want to hang him as quick as they can to keep it legal. Take care of it before somebody else decides to do it on their own."

Sloane gazed at the dancing image of the candle flame reflected against the windowpane. "I've been meaning to ask you something."

Hiram answered with his eyes alone.

"I've been meaning to ask you about what you seen. What it was really like. You know, over there in France."

The candle sizzled as the wax oozed a long tear on the windowsill. Hiram tossed off the rest of his liquor. "I'm about worn out, Daddy. It'll keep till another day."

Hiram leaned over and breathed on the candle. The flame wrung itself out and a thread of smoke traced a black wraith against the glass. Hiram raised the window to let it out.

Thirteen

Sloane went on to the courthouse alone. Even though there was much talk about the trial in town already, jury selection didn't attract much of a crowd. The routine formality of justice did not interest the mob. Only the promise of bloodshed could do that.

Sloane had asked Hiram if he wanted to come along, but his son was busy sending off another boy to the Marines and needed to make sure he didn't run off before he was safely on the train. It was just as well to be alone. Sloane needed to see this thing on his own and for himself.

The judge was a man named Buck L'Hommedieu. He was tall and thin with a knife-blade face and a peppered mustache waxed at each end like a comma. Even from nine pews deep in the courtroom, Sloane could smell the rich stench of hair pomade when the judge took his seat up in the pulpit. His gown hung from broad but stooped shoulders, tailing down behind the bench like the wings of a great black bird gone to roost.

Two men on the main floor stood from their tables

and came forward and began conferring with the judge in voices no one in the main gallery could hear. The straw-haired lawyer who'd interviewed Sloane remained seated, one leg languidly tossed over the other, a long, yellow pencil notched behind his ear. Sloane craned his neck to see if they'd brought Matt Vaughn in, but there was no evidence of any of the Vaughns anywhere throughout the courtroom. The only others present beside himself appeared to be those summoned for jury consideration.

The lawyers began calling names and the men stood and strolled forward. Most of them hadn't even bothered putting on suits, and as they passed, the dust from their work clothes rose and hung thick in the air, wheeling motes through strong beams of sunlight. After a while, the smell of sweat and leather was enough to chase away the stink of the judge's hair jelly.

The questions were the same. Most of the men confessed they knew the accused and were immediately dismissed from consideration. A few of the local business proprietors claimed no acquaintance. Their clothes were new and pressed, their accents from places beyond the high country. Some of these men were accepted. Many were not.

With the midday break Sloane took his lunch across the street at the rear of a drug store where canned sardines and crackers were sold with sweating bottles of Pepsi-Cola. Only a few men came and went. None lingered once they'd made their purchase and had it bagged in plain brown paper. Save one.

"Sloane Tobit, as I live and breathe."

Sloane swiveled on his stool, squinting hard at the face that regarded him. Old skin the color of slurry and copper whiskers. In profile a green eye cocked like a fish, bland and lunatic. Gant Cobb. A born stripe of trouble. Sloane hadn't seen him in nearly a decade and that last remembering revived no pleasant tidings. "Sit on down, Cobb."

"I figured you as much as a hermit as myself. What's drawn you out?"

"Old Matt, of course. Come to see what all this fuss is about." Cobb nodded to the clerk behind the counter and ordered a cup of tomato soup and some coffee. "Besides, it's my legal duty don't you know. I'm part of the summons."

Sloane nodded, studying the Eagle Claw fishing hooks hanging from a row of pegs behind the cash register.

"Well, they'll get rid of you soon as they know you and Matt know one another. They ain't about to stand for that, I can assure you."

Cobb scooted his tomato soup on the counter, the steam drawing up like plucked cobwebs. "Maybe. We'll see about that now, won't we?"

"What's that supposed to mean?"

Cobb gently sipped the soup from the edge of his spoon as if it were something to be breathed in with the greatest care, lest it spooked. "Means my memory ain't so good no more. Maybe all those hunting trips might not be so clear to my mind as they once were. In fact, I'm having a hard time recollecting if I even know you, old coon."

"I imagine the law had things to say about a man what would choose to forget a thing like what you're talking about."

"That right? Well, maybe that's so. Maybe too, folks from Sanction County has a few things to say about a man who could carve up his own blood kin."

Cobb was accepted into the jury pool late that afternoon,

the last to be seated. Sloane watched him shuffle out the side with the other appointed members and disappear somewhere into the anonymous hallways of their sequestration.

Sloane went to the boarding house and sat waiting in the dining room for the others to come in when it was time to eat. The widow found him there, staring out at the evening coming. "La, Mr. Tobit. I didn't know you were just sitting in the dark in here. Let me go fetch up some matches and shed some light."

"I don't mean to be no trouble, ma'am. I'm just setting."

"No trouble, Mr. Tobit. No trouble now."

He watched her glide out, a phantom on the light airs of her own enchantment. When she came back in and lighted the wicks, it looked like she was dolloping the magic of fire from some secret between her fingertips. She lifted the decanter of brandy from the sideboard and placed it on the long table, pouring out two neat glasses. "I want you to be comfortable."

He encircled his field-hardened fingers around the rim of the glass and drank.

"Albert told me he saw you at the courthouse this afternoon. I understood the trial hadn't started as yet."

"No ma'am, not yet. They just sit the members of the jury is all. The trial will begin tomorrow."

"I see. Well, I for one will be glad when it's up and over with. I had to turn away three of those little nasty ole newspapermen just this afternoon. I'm proud to give a man who needs it a room, but I'll not be party to the vulgar doings of such folks as that. That reminds me of something."

"Yes, ma'am?"

"It's just that, with there being a few rooms to spare and you and your son having to double up. What I'm saying is that I don't see any reason why you couldn't take advantage of the extra space. While you're testifying here at the trial, I mean. It's a real good room, I assure you, and a little bit of space never was took as untoward. No charge for it, of course. Not between friends. Here, I'll fetch the key straightaway while I'm thinking of it."

Before Sloane could utter a word, she popped from her seat and swept into the next room. She returned in only a moment, the thin bells of the key chain tolling her arrival.

"There now, let me slip that right there in your pocket." Her hand brushed his coat lapel to the side and placed the key in his breast pocket, the flat of her hand lingering briefly over his heart before she snatched it away. Then she did something so strange Sloane almost doubted his ears. She giggled. Sloane felt blood rise in his neck. She smiled and sat, sipping from her brandy once more.

They sat, speaking quietly for a few minutes until the front door opened and the few boarders, including Hiram, began strolling in. The widow excused herself, saying she would have to see everything set up right in the kitchen with Albert and encouraged Sloane to drink as much of her brandy as he wished.

Hiram pulled out the chair next to his father. "How you getting on, Daddy?"

"Fair to middling. They got the jury sat."

"That's what I heard." Hiram poured his own small glass of the brandy. "The sheriff came by and let me know that lawyer will probably be putting me up on the stand sometime tomorrow afternoon."

"That early?"

"That's what he claimed. Said they want me and Gerald Spenser to have our say out first. Get the eyewitnesses to what the body looked like. The others, the Price brothers and you, they mean to bring in toward the end."

"Any reasoning behind that?"

Hiram shrugged, waving his half-filled glass. The smell of the liquor traveled the room. "They think what you have to say is their best shot at putting the nail in the old man's coffin. They figure since you knew him and the girl both, it will make it more real to the jury. Not just a story about a crazy fool doing something nobody can fathom. But a man, an old friend, doing the absolute worst thing to his own child. If there's one thing that should demand conviction, it's that."

That night Sloane slept poorly in his room. Hiram's words at supper were sharp in his ear and the whole night seemed drawn down with the weight of the trial still coming. He tried drinking a little, but that only loosed old memories, none of them good. He crossed the room in his bare feet and stood gazing at himself in the room's only mirror, rubbing the few patches of whiskers he'd missed when he'd shaved. The blue cant of lunar light laid a stripe across his jaw, drawing the hidden gray whorls into eerie relief. His face had become a map, the spots of beard growth the topography of hidden mountains. He lightly ran his hands over his face. Under his fingers he could feel a whole country in masquerade.

He regretted selling the hooch runner the mirrors. Custom had it that when someone died the mirrors should be covered to keep the dead from looking back into the world. But when Nara killed herself, he'd not observed the tradition. In the time she'd been gone he felt like he sometimes glimpsed a shadow of her passing from one of the mirrors into the other. But now that they were gone, there was no way to invite the dead in. This mirror, the one he looked at now, it was unfamiliar. No one lived here.

Fourteen

When the jury entered from the side corridor, Sloane exchanged a look with Gant Cobb. He allowed a nod. Cobb grinned back. Sloane had thought of saying something to the lawyer about Cobb's lie that he did not know Matt Vaughn. It seemed wrong to let it go unchallenged. Wrong to allow a man to taint the rest of the jury with his own malicious will. But Sloane kept silent. Maybe some part of him agreed with Cobb. Cut off the infected limb and let it rot.

The courtroom quickly filled with all the good folk of the town. Sloane could hear them whispering their opinion of guilt or innocence while they reached over the backs of their seats to shake hands and swap hellos with their neighbors. All of them self-appointed members of the world's judiciary. Hiram came in wearing his marine uniform and sat next to his father. They didn't have a chance to wish one another good morning before Judge L'Hommedieu sharply rapped the gavel to call the court to order.

The prosecuting lawyer rose from his chair with a show

of great reluctance. His girlish face was bland and unconcerned and it looked as though he had no interest whatsoever in the business of earthly justice. He began to pace a line, sweeping his fine hair from his eyes with a little backhand brush, his bluebottle eyes raking the sitting members of the jury. He kept eying them for so long without saying a word that a couple of the men began to cough and tug at their neckties and shift in their seats. When the lawyer suddenly brought himself up short, the men's gazes fixed, their eyes drawn to him like metal filings to a magnet. He smiled brilliantly in the face of their attention. With their eyes following him, he strolled over to Matt Vaughn and pointed his yellow pencil at the old man's throat, holding it there as steady as a spear tip.

The lawyer began to talk. Sloane listened to some of it but the words grew stubborn and tangled and the lawyer's meaning was soon lost to him in errant trails of Latin and legal codes. The room drummed with the sound of the lawyer's empty speech. Sloane felt his breath come and go like a heavy train lumbering through his body. He clasped his hands on his lap and looked down, studying the crevices and details age had worn there in his flesh. He crawled down there among the folds of his joined hands, making himself snug and impossibly small, imagining a place and time he could understand.

A scream shattered the lawyer's droning and a chorus of gasps rippled through the court gallery. Matt Vaughn in his poorly fitting tan suit rose up from his chair, his pale and manacled fists wagging above his head. His lawyer worked his slab of a face into a grimace and sprang all in one motion, as if the force of his facial expression was the engine driving his physical strength. He grabbed hold of his client and wrapped him against his own chest, wrestling to keep the old man restrained.

"Be still now, goddammit, be still!" The defense attorney's face was the raspberry color of hard-pinched skin.

The judge hollered and whipped his gavel so hard that it slipped from his hand and went clattering across the pulpit. The defense attorney clamped his hands tight together, encircling Matt Vaughn's trunk and began to squeeze him hard, constricting his client. Vaughn's scream went a pitch higher and his legs thrashed the air like a man falling from a great height might seek a foothold in the final moments before he hit the ground.

Once they'd taken the crazy old man and locked him up for his and everyone else's benefit, they got around to the proper business of trying him. The defense attorney, his left eye bruised where Vaughn had struck him during his fit, talked about the good and moral life his client led up until the day he killed his daughter. The attorney had to know there was no fighting the conviction now. Not with the lunatic airs the old man obviously breathed. But there was still the matter of the sentence to be decided, the valuing of a man's whole life, and that could not be determined by considering a single act alone.

Hiram stood when his name was called and stepped up to the witness box. He laid his hand on the Bible and nodded when the bailiff asked him if his word was good. He didn't say anything. Neither the judge nor the lawyer seemed to notice. The oath of a war hero must have required no voiced promises.

When Hiram began to talk, Sloane could not keep from

seeing the things described even when he closed his eyes, the mind's darkness granting him no grace. The ripped skin. The slick intestines crawling over the dirt like bloody vines. The hair scattered and clotted with gore. The pieces of the child inside her, dismantled and strewn like a cast-off raggedy doll. Hiram spoke of the girl's torn body without a plug of emotion. His words issued the details matter-of-factly, expertly even, as if in some hidden space of his life he had mastered a surgeon's professional language. He told of suppurations and contusions and the manner by which they were likely inflicted with the confidence of a man who suffered no doubt about the subject under discussion. It was the talk of a man who understood the business of bloodletting.

With the court's adjournment, Sloane didn't seek Hiram's company. He hobbled through the lingering and chatting crowd and took the courthouse steps faster than he ought, narrowly missing a tumble. The pain along his backbone danced with each step he took, but he moved quickly on, eager to get as far away from the courtroom as he could.

He found the hotel tavern still empty in the late afternoon doldrums and crossed to a small table wedged into one of the darker nooks. The bartender wiped his hands on a small white towel before flinging it over his shoulder and laboriously circling around to take his order.

"I'll be needing something from around back." When Sloane spoke his tongue felt like a tobacco sheaf in his mouth.

The bartender stared down on him with rheumy and fractious eyes. "We got tea and coffee. We ain't got what you want. Nobody does."

Sloane scissored his chin between his fingers and blew out a laborious breath. "I know good and goddamn well you've got some liquor in this place. Now, go on and get me some."

The bartender looked on and blinked. "This ain't charity. Pay before and I'll see what there is."

Sloane ransacked his pockets and turned up a crumpled dollar. The bartender clutched it and went on through the swinging doors behind the bar. While he was gone Sloane stared down in the dim light at his hand spread palm down on the tabletop. He wasn't shaking, not yet, but he could feel the hot tremors coming on.

He was given a half-drained bottle of whiskey and a steel mug. He filled it himself and studied the wall opposite when the bartender went away. The whiskey was strong even though it had been watered down to the cloudy color of lemonade. It struck at his belly and solar plexus first, radiating up into his limbs before it lapped back to its hard, centered burn, only to expand again, moving recurrently through his body like a tide of sulfur and smoke and ease. He crushed his breath down small and held it pent, knowing the blood would drown the whiskey all too soon. He needed to drain what pleasure he could while he was able.

It became easier to think on the trial when he'd finished that first mug full, and easier yet with the second. He no longer had to stand sentinel in his mind against the siege of remembering. It came now in orderly ranks that could be dealt with in turn. The stark images were gone, floated away in the vapors of drinking. No more compositions inked with blood and brain.

Sloane was terrified of facing the judge and jury like Hiram had. The faces of the crowd gazing on him, all wanting to hear him sign the death warrant of a blind and incomprehensible creature beyond the pale of even something as universally loathed as evil. Sign it with speaking a testimony that he'd never seen such things in his humble life. Did they truly believe that was the way to name the price for a man's sinfulness? The price that all men must face eventually.

The sun was just beginning to go down when he finished the bottle. He left penniless by the front door. Only a few citizens were out, it being close to a civilized supper hour. He walked past a gaming hall, a few laconic snaps of pool balls upstairs denoting the casual play within, the establishment's windows thrown high to catch what benefit of breeze it could. He could hear the high-pitched laughter of an old woman tickling the smoky air. He stopped and stared up at the voice, the shadowed square and the dim suggestion of movement inside. Who could say what might draw this invisible woman away from her proper attention to a household of children or grandchildren? Perhaps old women owned secrets that did not bear easy revelation. Perhaps old men knew better than to try to guess.

His head felt light. If the cool of the evening was respite, the brassy dance of sunset on the enclosing mountain range was not. He eased himself to the curb, his hip joints cracking as he folded into a seated position and leaned forward on his cane. A butterfly beating pulsed behind his eyes when he looked on the coruscating ridgelines. Even when he closed his eyes to the last vestige of the day's leaving, he could feel the animal throb coming so rapidly it seemed his lids would fly open like snapped window shades and his eyeballs would pop like flashbulbs.

A pair of men passed, their stroll quickening as they

neared him. As they went on, he could hear their young laughter curling back to him in a thinly veiled taunt.

The sputum rose first and then the bile, plashing on the dirt and drilling a parti-colored sinkhole in the soft ground. He dropped the cane and coughed. His numb fingers pinched his nose and he blew out what mucus there was. He sat panting, his elbows on his knees, his hands lifted to the sky in a transparent pillory.

It was full on dark before he could stand. Once he did, he stumped off on in an arbitrary direction, his eyes not lifting at anyone he passed. He heard only voices and tittering and he wished them all as old and broken as he.

He woke the next morning in a yard thick with billy goats. The animals stilt-walked round his prostrate form, clapping wary gold eyes on him and defecating with contempt. He rose on one elbow to better survey his environs and saw a gate slightly ajar and a dirt trail that seemed vaguely familiar to his drink-diluted memory. Some of the goats had butted their way through the unlocked gate and were breakfasting on the neighboring lawn. A wooden mailbox was fixed there, the name "Sluder" painted in white.

He cast round for his walking stick and, with a great sinking weight in his belly, he saw it clamped between the jaws of a gray and grizzled specimen in the corner of the pen. He was bigger than the other goats and his horns were shaped out of symmetry, one curling down over his eye like a cowlick. Along his coarse-haired stomach was a dark stain where he'd lain there in the mud and pissed himself. Sloane stood to a chorus of quarrelsome bleats and came shaking his fist at the old goat. The beast glanced up disinterestedly while it continued to worry the cane.

Sloane backed off, seeing the goat had no intention of ceding his prize with a mere display. He spoke to it. It flapped its ear once while it continued to stubbornly gnaw. The wood began to splinter and drip from its jaws in pieces the size of ticks. Sloane grew furious and shouted, drawing out another truculent round of bleating from the population at large but nothing from the bedded gray.

Grabbing hold of the cane on each side of the goat's working mouth, Sloane wrested up on one end while pressing down with the other, trying to break the torque, but the goat simply craned its neck a few degrees, as if the animal mistook this attack for harmless game. Only when Sloane delivered a hard kick to the goat's chest did the stakes raise.

The goat lunged to its hooves with great speed, coming out of its languid pose with muscles coiled and tight. The blow was so sudden and great and caught Sloane so low in his center of gravity that he was flung back several feet, his brogans streaking through raw manure. The goat tossed its head and made a muffled blat, its teeth not daring to let go of its property. Sloane saw the white hotness of hate. "Gimme that stick, you goddamn goat!"

The beast cut its shoulder toward the fence line and trotted straight through a gathering of pawing onlookers, lifting its head so it could pass freely among them without catching the cane in their horns. They dipped and bowed as the gray goat stopped in the center of their numbers. They all stood looking at Sloane, flicking their ears.

He advanced, waving his arms in wide carousel circles. For a moment, the front rank balked, but as he reached over their backs to get at one end of the walking stick, the whole formation broke away as if a single body, a rippling obstacle of hood and hide moving in gentle concert, so that the gray goat remained safely beyond his reach. He tried different angles of approach, growing more breathless and infuriated with each failed attempt.

Then it came to him. He spat and nodded to himself, figuring that it would have to work. He backed away from their collected numbers and ignored them as he leaned against the palings on the far side of the pen. He looked at them and spread his arms out at either side, braced by the fence line, looking for all the world as unconcerned about the cane as he possibly could. The wall of goat flesh watched him with unblinking eyes. He clapped his hands and whistled and still they moved not a jot. "That's about what I figured."

He stepped across a few feet, his shoe soles sucking mud as he went, and placed his palm against the pen's wooden frame gate. It yawned all the way back and clapped lightly against the outer palings. The way out was unblocked. "Now, you all think 'bout that for a minute."

The goats sidled and some few took steps towards the opposite side of the pen. Sloane went back to where he'd stood before and leaned lackadaisically against the palings. The animals started testing him, dancing out a few feet from the herd to see if he showed any interest. He continued to look blandly on. "Ain't nothing keeping you."

The pressure against the dam was too much. A black goat with a white star between its eyes was the first to break from the herd. He took a few mincing steps forward and then broke into a full trot, passing unscathed into the greater pasture beyond. Sloane turned his head and watched the billy goat go, whistling but not stirring from where he reclined. Next came a pair of identical tans with dirty yellow stockings. They exited side by side, crossing the gateway like a matched team of horses or mules. Once they cleared the passage, though, they split off in individual directions, bleating and capering with carnival joy. Then they joined one another once more and playfully touched horns, pressing their weight against one another in a recreational sparring match.

The others came singly and in pairs. Only the stubborn gray remained standing inside the pen. Sloane sighted him down for a good long while. He could almost swear he could see the images of the other frolicking beasts reflected in the goat's yellow eye. The gray bleated, baring his teeth, but still would come no closer to the way out. Sloane swore quietly and expertly and came staggering, swinging his hands in openhanded gestures, fanning the air with his stark white palms. The gray angled away, retreating on its stiffened haunches, measuring itself in relation to the diminishing room for maneuver. With the palings drawing in ever closer, the goat tossed its head and made a dash, loosing its joints in gallop for the gateway.

The stick slammed against the staves. The goat strained up against the fence line, the tip of its muzzle poking into the wide open space of the pasture, but its trunk and legs barred from exit by the very object it hoarded. It backed away and butted forward once more, the fence trembling from the violence of the blow, the cane still clutched tightly in its mouth.

Sloane could see the goat's eyes rolled skyward, fixed and insolent in a moment of paralysis. He gripped it by its one good horn and tugged its head up so that they could stare at one another. "Drop the goddamn thing."

The goat bleated back loud and long and defiant.

"All right, then."

Sloane dropped his free hand in his trouser pocket, opened the clasp knife, and passed the blade across the gray's quivering windpipe in a single motion. The animal's fight went out suddenly and it bucked and pitched its whole body, the sticking flinging high and disregarded. Sloane let go the goat's horn and flattened himself against the fence palings while the goat slung itself about the pen in a lunatic dance of its own finality. Once he was sure he was clear, Sloane ducked out the gate to where the cane lay and took it and did not glance back in the pen. He could hear the goat still wallowing, but there was nothing to be done about that now. He moved off, limping past the yard full of loose goats. He shook his head at hearing them make such a blathering ruckus as he went. They couldn't have had the first idea in the world where they were headed.

Fifteen

That evening Sloane learned his absence at court on the second day went largely unnoticed. Hiram told him when he'd come up bearing a few scraps from supper. Sloane had managed to slip into his room earlier without drawing the widow's eager attention and moved over the floorboards in socked feet to remain undetected. But Hiram knew he'd be in and stood tapping outside the door for several minutes before Sloane finally got up and answered. "I ain't testifying."

"That right?" Hiram pushed the door open with one hand while extending the plate of ham hock and turnip greens, the steam and smell wafting up. He crossed the room and set the plate on the empty desk and stood looking out the back window at the empurpled evening making a pretty picture of the rundown backyard. He raised the pane and placed a cigarette between his lips but did not yet light it. Wind seesawed the drapes.

"You might have some explaining to do if you don't

go on up to the courthouse and say your piece about Matt Vaughn."

Sloane watched his son in profile, the unlit cigarette angled from his mouth. It reminded him of a sideshow trick he'd seen once of a sharpshooter who'd snipe the silver ash off a volunteer's smoke with a .22 and still leave the cherry burning.

Sloane took a bite of the greens and set the fork down. "I don't figure I've rightly got it in me, Son."

Hiram cocked one eye at him but didn't move his head. He lowered himself onto the windowsill and shielded a match-strike with his cupped palm until the cigarette bled thin wires of smoke as fleeced and fine as cotton stranded in briar.

"It doesn't matter that he was your friend, you know? That doesn't matter once you go off and do something like that."

"Hell, that don't have nothing to do with it."

"What does, then?"

A door opened and closed at the end of the hallway and a shuffling pair of boots came by, crunching grains of house dust underfoot. Sloane waited for it to pass by and clack down the stairs before he said anything.

"I don't want to have to do what you did." His eyes journeyed the length of the floor. "I don't want to have to have my say out in court like that. It don't feel right, not with what I done to Kite. How can I get up there and tell on a man for killing his own when I done the same myself?"

Hiram remained silent for a very long time, his face turned to the darkness on the other side of the window. "You've got to do it, Daddy. You just owe it, is all."

He combed his hair well and brushed the suit clean and went straight to the courthouse with the sun full and bright. Hiram had already gone ahead to speak with the lawyer to make arrangements for his father to wait in one of the building's offices until it was time to testify. That was the one concession Sloane had drawn out of his son. Do this thing, yes, but do it with patience and a deliberate mind. He still expected that dignity.

The room was clean and spare, unused. A tall casement window overlooked a spread of honeysuckle curling in on itself with bees threading the loops and tangles of the crazy vine script, repeatedly thumping themselves against the windowpane. There wasn't much of a view beyond that. Only the climbing green of a hill that shut off clear sight of the town and what it held.

A young man in a blue serge suit came in every half hour to check on him and refill his water glass. Sloane couldn't believe how thirsty he'd become in the waiting room. It recalled a depletion as complete as his body had known at a day's end of hard field labor. But that thirst, that need, resulted from an appreciable exertion. This was different. This was a clutching strangeness inside his body, a vague cancer that suckered every drop of moisture. As he drank, the chilled water brought no relief, but only briefly softened the inevitable pain growing sharp and tight within the rings of his throat.

Late in the morning, Hiram stepped in to check on him. There was nothing to report. The Price brothers were still being questioned.

"How you holding up?"

Sloane thought. "Holding."

Hiram let slip a slow grin and sat in one of the two chairs, his wide palms resting on his knees.

"How much longer will it be, Son?"

Hiram lifted his hands weakly, uncertain. He offered his father a cigarette, and for once Sloane took it. The paper felt odd between his lips, crisp and neutral, but when he inhaled he could taste the smoke going deep as a drain. His blood rose. He hacked and smiled.

"Maybe I done myself no favors by discounting this baccy. It might not beat a cigar but it carries more than it should."

Once they finished, Hiram asked if he was interested in taking lunch at the hotel when the midday break arrived. Sloane declined, saying he'd have to stay where he was until he was summoned to the courtroom, otherwise he might not be around when his name was called before God and man. He added that he was glad to see the room they'd put him in had the window nailed shut. "Boxed in like a bridegroom."

Hiram smiled at that and said he'd see him soon.

As the hours passed, the missed meal barely registered in Sloane's guts. The welt of hunger was no great concern to his soul, and on his soul his thoughts single-mindedly dwelled. He prayed to God, but he knew God suffered no selfishness in these matters. The silence did not surprise him. Then he spoke to Nara and Kite. If they heard, neither of their voices was allowed reply.

The room grew large and stark and mysterious. Space, like time, had begun to divide from itself, and in this new absence vast horizons of emptiness were springing up, unfolding into an expansive nothing. His body and mind were part of it, his soul too. All of it gone thin and insubstantial as a thought. Even his limbs seemed a universe away. His head felt like it was smoke running up a chimney and his feet like the dirt-starved roots of the largest tree in the world. He spoke his name aloud. Again and again, as if willing himself into singularity.

A moment later, the polite young man tapped at the door and said it was time for him to take the witness stand. Sloane looked at him, blinking his eyes, then rose and followed him down the corridor.

He moved down to the witness stand and took the few steps up without the aid of his cane. He'd forgotten his walking stick in the room, but he felt uncrippled for the moment and did not notice its loss. The bailiff came with the Bible and Sloane swept his hand over its heavy black cover and agreed to speak true to his own word. Many of the general public in the courtroom whispered loudly to one another. So much so that the judge struck his gavel three times and told the good folk of Sanction County and the Fourth District to behave themselves or risk removal. Sloane sat.

He'd not seen her when he entered, but hers was the first tallowy face his eyes happened to light upon once seated on the stand. Ruth Vaughn, the victim's mother and accused's wife. She sat alone. No one, not a single member of her larger family was with her. Even strangers had sidled with intent when they discovered through courtroom gossip who she was, frightened by her as one might be by an infection. She did not dip her head nor lower her eyes when the lawyer stepped forward to ask Sloane his questions. It was as though she wanted to gage every gesture and exchange, every small hesitation between incriminating words, to judge for herself if what was being said of her evil husband

and dead daughter was truly real and not happening to some other woman ghosted by the fog of her own madness.

Sloane waited for the pause in the prosecuting attorney's questions before he spoke. The answers he gave were quick and simple and followed a natural order. He recounted the details of his decades-long association with Vaughn and his family, the crease of memory running a row as neat as a plow line. He remembered Vaughn as most would remember him: hardworking and proud and a fine hand for turning a profit despite lean harvests. Like many others, he was just a native son and nothing more. Until that day.

Then there was the discovery of the girl. The attorney spared Sloane the details, instead settling for his testimony that he had been present when the posse discovered Vaughn and his crime. He spoke of having seen the blood on his old friend's hands. He told what it was like to look on what little remained of the poor daughter's body, the child killed for the child inside her. The attorney closed his eyes in a moment of sanctity, thanked him, said some words to the judge, and turned to take his seat. Sloane braced himself for the defense attorney's cross-examination. His fingers templed in his lap.

"I have no questions, your Honor."

He thought he'd heard wrong and so he sat still. Disbelief pinned him to the witness stand like a stone. Was it possible that they would not question his word? How could they not? How could they let him go with so little of this wicked life resolved? The judge reiterated the pardon, speaking the words softly as one might to a child, and Sloane rose on uncertain legs, leaving the stand and the courtroom as if he'd just stepped onto a time-strewn and alien continent. The doors yawned open into the blazing white town.

He was not present at the conviction and sentencing. That was a time for the newspaper reporters running like some virulence without principle or prejudice, asking all those involved what it was like to witness the blind gaze of justice. Three days had passed since his testimony and still it was hard for Sloane to imagine he'd spoken before the judge and jury and not faltered. In that time he'd continued taking his meals alone in his room. He had not made preparations to leave though he had no true cause keeping him in town. Perhaps it was his evening talks with Hiram. He'd come to enjoy and even look forward to them.

It was the widow who told Sloane what was to be done with old Matt Vaughn. They were taking him to the state penitentiary. There was to be no death sentence. No one seemed to know why or why not, but that was the seal arbitrarily placed on this sad state of affairs. Everyone in town seemed glad to let it rest at that and simply go on without troubling their hearts over it any longer, forgetfulness being a more dependable remedy for this sort of thing than forgiveness. A rumor about town had it that Sloane's testimony might have done something to save the old man's life by casting a friendlier light on a man who might easily have been judged as a monster. Sloane doubted what he said made the slightest difference, but there were worse things to take credit for in this life, he decided.

The widow further said that they held a late funeral for Martha Vaughn at the church cemetery. Word had to be sent to bring in all of the far-flung kin and it had been held the day after the conviction. Some newsmen had stood outside the gates to the burying ground and asked Ruth Vaughn was it worse to lose a daughter to the grave or a husband to the devil. She spit on them and said nothing.

That same night when the widow Stark told him these things, the two of them went out and sat alone on the front porch, their faces turned to the surprisingly cool evening breeze blowing in. Sloane observed that a violent rain was likely to stripe the dust before midnight came. The widow agreed, rocking in her chair.

A long while passed before she spoke. "It's not that I don't know about your boy, Mr. Tobit." Her eyes did not move from the humped clouds breasting the valley.

He looked at her. "Don't know about what, ma'am? Me and Hiram might have bad blood, but blood still sticks. What lies has that boy been telling?"

She did not turn her eyes from the approaching weather. "Not Hiram, Mr. Tobit. Not Hiram."

He slumped back in his chair, feeling the air abruptly sucked away from him. Immediately he remembered the pain in his back. "I better be getting on to bed, then. I'm feeling a mite poorly." He rose.

"But it doesn't matter, Mr. Tobit. Don't you see? It doesn't matter to anyone anymore. Not to those that have lived and suffered and that understand. Only loss can know and understand loss."

"It's been a long day and I'm awfully tired."

He took a step towards the door. Her hand gripped his wrist. "Because who knows why these things happen? Even if God does, it's only in his mind. That's not the same as what we people of skin and bone feel. Not the same. Even though I love God and pray to him, I don't think he really understands what I go through every morning. How could he? How could he, being at such a distance? That's not blasphemy, that's just living."

He made to draw away but she held on to him.

"Don't tell me you haven't asked why man has to pay the price he does for being born into this world, Mr. Tobit! You know in your heart that's all there is ever to worry about in this life. Don't you go on up there to your cabin in the woods by yourself and pretend there's not more to your sorrow than what you or me or anyone on this green Earth will ever understand."

With his free hand he pried her hands off and strode inside, the screen door clapping shut behind him. Even when he mounted the stairs and moved down the hall, he couldn't help but hear her soft words repeated.

Sixteen

Hiram persuaded Sloane to stay on at the boarding house a few more days despite his assertion that he must be getting on. Hiram explained there were only a few loose ends in town he needed to attend to and then he would ride back with his father, bringing along provisions enough to get the old man through the fall and the first part of the winter. Sloane was more than capable of seeing to his own welfare, but the promise of company on the ride back lured him into agreement.

Sloane avoided the downstairs of the house completely, not wishing to repeat the scene with the widow. He knew she meant well by what she'd tried to say to him and he suspected if there was another human who could understand the white hell of loneliness it was her. But he was not strong enough to tear up the fallow grounds of his past. Not with a woman wallowing in great open fields of her own private regret. Not with anyone at all. Maybe that's what true loneliness was—not being able to explain what pain you suffered, even to those who most wanted to share and solace it.

When they finally did leave it was by the dimmest light of morning, the night just beginning to recede into its own shadow colors. Albert had been up and saddled both the gray horse and Sloane's tired mule. Sloane shook the boy's hand and thanked him for his hospitality and asked him to convey the same sentiments to his kind mother.

"Yes, sir, Mr. Tobit. Pleasure having you. You come on again whenever the fancy strikes."

When Hiram came along and they both straddled their mounts and turned out of the small stable, Sloane remembered all those years ago when they'd rode together a full day to hunt deer at the old camp. Only now, Hiram sat a bit higher than his father and led the way.

Because it was still somewhat dark and sleep heavy on his mind, Sloane didn't immediately realize his son was leading him not away from town but to its center. As he rode, Sloane watched Hiram from the tail of his eye. He did not ask where they were going. He had come to believe that there was something to be said for a father who willingly followed his son.

They turned single-file down one of the back alleys, the leaning fence lines dimly flanking their passage. The yards on either side were cramped and noisy with dogs and chickens. No townsmen were out yet, still just shades on the other side of the yellow window squares. Save one. The Sluder boy, standing at the gate of the last little plot along the row, all alone except for his cigarette and scowl.

Sluder spoke to Hiram, not bothering to remove the butt from his lips. "I'll thank ye to keep that mean son-of-a-bitch as far away from me as you please."

Hiram looked round at his father then back to the boy. "I paid you for your time, not your goddamn mouth."

The boy spat the cigarette into the mud and climbed up in the saddle with Hiram. They turned out at the end of the alley. As Sloane rode past Sluder's yard he could see it was emptied of billy goats.

Once they were clear of Canon City and had cut up the causeway to the high trails, Hiram nudged the gray horse aside to let Sloane pass him on the path.

"Take us on home, Daddy."

They didn't get in until it was full dark and all three were exhausted beyond words. Hiram put the animals up to rest and none of them bothered with fire or meal. Sloane showed Hiram some bedding they could make up on the floor and then he closed the bedroom door and sat on the edge of the bed staring out the viewless window hoping he would not lose heart now. He spoke Nara's name and then Kite's and then he slept.

Hiram woke him early with a cup of coffee and they agreed to drink it on the front porch while Sluder still slept, not to spare the boy the noise of their waking but to simply take in the morning together. They did not exchange more that a few dozen words but the silences were companionable and without meaning. The sun slumbered long in the tree branches and the morning birds crossed their dark bodies across the fractured light. Cool shadows slanted an elaborate wirework across the yard. The coffee cooled in the men's mugs while they watched and listened and waited for the cold purpose of this day to come.

Sluder leaned out from the doorway, his suspenders lowered around his waist and his hair stiff with filth. "Let's get this done so we can head back. I got no use for this place."

The boy clumped back inside to retrieve some article or perhaps merely punctuate his disdain.

They all stepped out into the yard together. Sloane's back was fine this morning and he went without his walking stick. He and Hiram trailed behind Sluder, following at his heels like hunters behind a prize hound, the boy's face turned toward the ground.

"This here is the spot. Go and roll your stones out here while I'm standing at it."

"That's not how it works. Keep an eye on him, Daddy. I'll be right back."

Hiram moved off around to the other side of the house. When he came back a minute later, he had a pair of spades shouldered like fowling pieces.

Sluder let out a breath. "Ah, hell. I know you're good and damn crazy."

Hiram tossed one of the spades handle first toward Sluder. The boy stepped aside and let it clatter untouched at his feet.

"You better pick that thing up and set to digging. It's a long walk back to Canon City."

Sluder looked at the shovel for a moment before he bent over and grabbed the handle like he meant to strangle it.

They dug with the benefit of a cloud-patched sky and a regular northern breeze. For much of the morning Sloane watched and offered to spell either of them, but Hiram refused out of consideration and Sluder out of pride. At noon, seeing there was nothing he could do but stand and watch the exhumation under the eerily fine weather, Sloane left them to their work and went down to the creek.

The shade was so deep along the bank that some stretches of the watercourse disappeared altogether in freshets of shadow so that the creek appeared as a chain running crooked and partial and hectic in the glancing sunlight. Sloane removed his shoes and stepped down into the creek on one of the strands firm with pebbles and sand and walked cautiously upstream, the current sucking his trouser cuffs tight to his naked ankles. He peered under logs for indication of trout but saw nothing but the muddied snouts of knobby heads. He slogged on.

It took only a few minutes of patient work to find the little tongue of driftwood-strewn ground projecting midway into the stream. He hadn't made a visit to this spot in some time, but the way here was a suture in his memory and he could never truly unbind it from his mind. His feet were just slim enough to pass between nested vine and turned roots littering the ground thickly. He staggered once, nearly turning his ankle against a stob, but still managed to pick his way through until he was clear of the beached detritus and up the rolling bank. Once he crested the berm, he sat and replaced his shoes and walked along the cane-hidden corridor. Its shuttered light probed the dark in little oval wounds, riddling his body.

He stepped up to the tiny clearing and squatted, looking at the solid embankment of rhododendron that he knew blocked his path to the house. To the left grew a wall of cane thick as a beard and to the right a logjam where the water slide was deep and gently boiling, bordered only by a thin paring of sand and beyond that a jungle of honeysuckle. There was no other way in. He'd been careful to see to that over the years. Before him were nine river rocks, worn round and precise, laid out on the ground and half buried in the smooth earth in the shape of a cross.

"Good morning, Son."

He swatted at a mosquito that had already attached to the back of the neck and drew his hand away to see his own blood mingling with the thorax. He could feel the welt rising.

"We're looking for your Momma today." His words sounded like wrinkles of thunder in his ears though he spoke nothing above the faintest whisper. "So if she's disturbed, you let me know." He stared down at the impassive stones. "All right, then. Don't worry. We'll be giving her back to you directly." He touched the center stone and stood on creaking joints and began his slow way back downstream.

With the last rumor of sunlight just showing, Hiram drove the spade tip into the hollow spot in the ground. All three men stopped and looked at one another, knowing they'd found what they were looking for.

Sluder broke the silence. "I told you all."

Hiram fixed him with a look and said nothing.

"You want time alone with her, Son?"

Hiram nodded once and Sloane told Sluder to follow him back to the house. The boy showed no inclination to listen, but neither did he seem intent on loitering in graves. He followed Sloane back, kicking at dust as he went.

Nearly an hour passed before Hiram called for Sloane, summoning him out alone. Father and son stood together, gazing down at the cool walls of the excavation, the depressed surface of the coffin lid.

"You wanted to know what it was like."

Sloane glanced up. "What what was like?"

Hiram met his father's eyes. "The war. The dying. It was like this. A neat place in the dirt that needed something you couldn't give it. No matter how bad it hurt it was always there, waiting, hungry for you. For some reason you couldn't explain, you kept running from it, even though you knew if you gave yourself up, all the pain would go away. But there was no way you could keep from running, keep living, even if you knew it was the last thing you wanted to do."

Sloane eased himself into a squat, palming a fistful of loose earth that he then flung over the coffin with a high, hard rattle, a flat rhythmic scattering that was like music shucked from a clapperless bell. "Lord, Son. Every wicked man on this Earth knows that."

Despite Sluder's noisome protest, it was too late to leave that night. To demonstrate his outrage, the foolish boy refused to sleep another godforsaken minute in that house and made up his bed next to a small fire by the creek. Had it been a month later than it was the evening chill would have likely driven him back to the comforts of the hearth, hospitable or otherwise. But the weather was entirely pleasant and neither Hiram nor Sloane bemoaned the absence of the boy's company. They contentedly took their evening meal of beans and whiskey on the front porch, listening to the summer night and talking to one another with unaccustomed ease.

It was quite some time in this strange country of agreement before Sloane changed the mood of the conversation. "I guess it's fair to say this family has always been split. Hacked right down the middle. That how it was when you were a young'un. Kite was his momma, through and through. You might not remember back that far, but when you were little bitty you was as much me as any feller could suffer. Always wanting to ride out and learn how to ride and plow and shoot. If you remember."

"I do. I remember it well enough."

The lunar light brushed the treetops, etching their outer shape against the dark.

"It was never my meaning that you should take after me. I wouldn't have wished it on anyone." When Sloane said that, he was certain a truer word had never passed his lips.

He watched Hiram tack the horse in the early light and offered to put together some spartan meal for the ride back but his son refused, saying he had enough to get to town with what he already carried in dry goods. They concurred that the weather would be fair for the journey and should pose no hazards. Hiram said he was pleased to look forward to the prospects of a quiet and scenic ride for once, smiling a little shyly at this. Sloane talked aimlessly even though there was nothing now to keep Hiram from leaving. He punched his hands in his pockets, exercising his voice like an athlete flexing old muscles, discovering the familiar qualities of speaking with no mind for how the words might be misheard, knowing that his intent was regarded with kind and forgiving ears. Eventually though, his words ate themselves up and father and son were left standing and looking off at the wind-bowed grass grown tall and pallid at the tips.

Hiram nodded once to Sloane and gained the saddle. "Don't be a stranger, Daddy. You know where I hang my hat."

"All right, then."

He turned the gray horse out towards the creek, presumably on his way to collect the boy Sluder. He had trotted but a few feet before he wheeled back and sat looking over the mountain range. It was pretty, lovely in fact, but nothing he hadn't looked on thousands of times before. Sloane waited to see what was keeping him.

"I mean to make Cass my wife."

"That right?"

Hiram affirmed that it was.

"Where you figure on living?"

The horse stepped, but Hiram did not take his eyes from the distant vista. "I don't see a reason to move her out of her own house. The place agrees with me well enough."

"You got a date fixed for this marrying?"

"The first of November."

Sloane likewise turned his gaze to the blue mountains, a lone spur of cloud poised over the split ridgeback. "That's your momma's birthday."

"Yes, sir, it is. There's nothing keeping you from coming down to hear the vows. If you're of a mind." Hiram turned the horse for good then and was gone.

He managed a late patch of squash and a few greens to ease his way into the long winter waiting and canned them before the first frost of mid-October. On good days he split enough wood to keep the cabin if not warm at least habitable. He went to the creek banks early each morning to monitor the fresh-laid tracks of deer, cat, and coon, and even shot a small six-point buck he gut-stripped and skinned after he'd hung it from a convenient oak limb. The venison complimented the boiled yellow squash as pretty as you could ask for.

With the onset of autumn he remembered Hiram's wedding. There were some days he was convinced there was no possible tickle of fate that could keep him away when the day arrived. But then sometimes the memory of pain lying dormant would shiver up his backbone and he feared the idea of darkening Hiram's doorway would be the worst thing he could do, both for his son and himself. The first of November came. Then it passed and Sloane was left to worry about his obligations no more, settling instead into a kind of resigned and numb disappointment.

The hard business of survival got even harder that year. What snow came was light, but the cold bottomed out that winter worse than he could ever remember. He often found himself wakened in the middle of the night and his breath coming in great ragged clouds. He would have to stir and build up the banked fire in the next room, the energy of his exertion likely generating more heat than the flames did. After several nights of this interruption, he dragged his bed ticking out to the main room and slept just inches from the grate. Even then he rarely slept through a night when the cold didn't wake him like some old nightmare.

During the days he hunted for stones. He meant to find nine more pieces identical to the ones marking Kite's grave. Hiram had marked Nara's resting place with a simple wooden cross before riding back to town, but Sloane knew she should have the solidity of rock to commemorate her passing. Something as permanent as the scar her death made on him.

He waded in the creek despite the cold, plunging his hands into the ice-girded stream. He must have handled hundreds of river rocks for each one he accepted. There were days when he came back to the cabin with gray-cold and empty hands and fell asleep by the fire. Sitting there he would dream of wondrous drifts of perfect stones pouring fourth from a hole in the sky like God's own bones.

The new year found him with his nine stones planted over Nara. It was only then he felt like her grave had been properly closed. He waited for many days to hear any discontent from any spirits thereabouts, but they remained silent and he figured the task done well.

The spring warming was gradual but any slight relief carried a small eruption of joy throughout the mountains. Bears were seen once more. Different birds too, winging back with their pitched squawks and cries. Sloane allowed himself walks beyond Black's Creek. Sometimes he carried his ancient shotgun as an excuse. If asked what he was about he could claim to be hunting, though in truth he went to enjoy the greater world coming to flower.

After one of these excursions, Sloane decided to brew himself a pitcher of spiced tea. He had walked further than normal and his muscles were tight with oncoming ache. Nara had always prescribed the homebrewed physic for any ailment of body or soul and Sloane had suffered these ministrations with amused tolerance. Now though it was the body itself that craved the remembered comfort, and there was nothing unfeigned in his desire for the tea.

He rummaged through all the cupboards looking for where she'd kept her brewing instruments. Somehow he'd forgotten where it was stashed, not having sought out anything weaker than whiskey in the time since her death. He remembered then she kept her leaves and china on the bottom shelf of the otherwise bare pie safe. He stooped down and ran his hand back where the space had gone foggy with cobwebs, his hands filming over with dusty time as he reached through. He froze when his fingers grazed the cool whisper of metal. It was not the simple clay pitcher he expected to find, but the smooth silver run of her teakettle. His private wedding gift to her all those years and pains gone. The one she'd said was the finest thing anyone could ever give her because it came from a place of honest and quiet but not sentimental love. Drawing it out, he saw it remained untarnished despite the long interval of neglect. When he held it to the light and saw his attenuated reflection blurring the surface, a single hot tear stung his cheek.

Sloane left in the middle of the night because he decided the moon was bright enough to safely light the way. He also wanted to have enough of an early start to arrive in Canon City by noon. The mule disagreed, though there was no telling if the beast's discontent owed more to the dark or the ungodliness of the hour. Three times it ducked the bit and tossed its head and kicked. Sloane punched it once, and when that did no good, he wrapped his arms around its neck and eared it until all the useless fight was gone. Then victor and vanquished rode on out.

Traveling at night pleased Sloane. The trails and the rocks that marked them felt under the mule's easy canter not like material objects of the physical world so much as renderings of these things, light counterfeits of a harsher reality still to be reckoned. The unsparing demands of everyday fact diminished with the vanishing of the yellow sun. The blue cool world spread over the land like breathable water and he was grateful to fill his lungs with it.

He missed his midday deadline for raising the town by a little over an hour and found the square relatively empty in the early afternoon of the workday. His belly was empty, but he had no money to pay for a meal and had already eaten what little salted venison he'd packed. Besides, he knew it would be easy to think himself into a fool if he didn't get on and get this done.

It took him some time to find the right trail. Forgetfulness was an angry and bitter root these days, worming down into his memory so that he could never be sure what was part of the world he accurately recollected and what was only shade. But he did find it, riding up slow past the one cabin where Cass's father was supposed to live and on to the house he remembered from that one kindly supper invitation.

He did not bother tying the mule and went up the stairs with the teakettle clutched to his chest. Standing and sweating there for a moment, he wondered what evil turn of whim had made him consider coming on this errand a good idea. Then, not having a choice nor the inclination to wait there for the rest of the day, he knocked.

He could hear sounds within, the pleasant raucous shuffling of feet across the tongue-in-groove flooring. Then the doorway dimmed and Sloane found himself standing face to face with his son. He awkwardly pressed the kettle into Hiram's arms. "It was something of your momma's. I figured you and yours might make use of it."

Hiram turned the silver piece in his hands. "I guess I should thank you."

"No, I don't figure so."

Over Hiram's shoulder, Sloane saw Cass and Note inside, busied over a loom, their fingers entwined in the intricate patterns still making. The little girl looked up and waved a pale hand in welcome.

Hiram stepped aside. "You eat anything?"

"I don't want to be a bother."

"We got leftovers, still warm in the pot."

"I should be getting back."

"There ain't no hurry."

Sloane worried his hat's brim between fingertips. "All right, then."

The womenfolk ushered him in with warm flutters of attention, coaxing the old man into the easy trappings of the afternoon's domestic comforts. They asked if they could fetch up anything to ease the discomfort of his journey, patting his dusty shoulders and hanging his old shapeless hat on the door peg. Hiram went out to secure the old mule. Sloane fidgeted under their ministrations.

Cass smiled. "It's right fine you've made the trip down, Mr. Tobit. My daddy's coming to evening supper. I've always held to the notion you and Daddy would get along fine."

Sloane shifted. "Why sure, I should be getting back though. I don't want to cause any problems. I was just here to bring something is all."

His eyes traveled to Cass's middle. He could see Hiram had written a new shape on her, a pleasant swelling at her hips and belly. She followed his gaze there and folded her hands against the life dozing inside.

"Hiram said he was meaning to tell you right soon."

Sloane stared long at the love scratched there. "Why... that's something else. I wouldn't have dreamed it. No, sir, not in all my years."

That evening was a fine suppertime of talking and remembering. Cass proved that indeed Sloane found much in common with the old widower Virgil, and both men were amazed to have lived so long in such proximity without ever having the pleasure of the other man's friendship. And while Hiram never made mention of the child his young wife carried, the old men exchanged a silent mutual congratulations, a blood pride that the separate tributaries of their family lines should converge into the broad currents of the future. An understanding passed between them, rending any veil of social awkwardness, and now their silver laughter came easily, as that of old comrades relieved to have been reunited after a despairing solitude. There was no hesitation in the things they said—how could there be, now that the family was warmly ensconced about them, securing the hierarchy of their age—no, there was only the natural mesh of what it meant to sit and share the assurance of some infinite reach beyond what could ever be expressed in simple words. That and the peace that descended over the comfort of true kinship.

It was getting on late, too late, before Sloane excused himself from the table and claimed his need to make his way back to Black's Creek. All, Hiram included, voiced their insistence that he not tramp the paths and trails at such an hour. Whatever magic of agreement was born that night in that moment, what mattered was that Sloane gave himself to it, saying that yes, perhaps they were right. Perhaps he could grace his threshold a day later than this. He could abide a night among these good people.

After he'd hugged Cass and Note good night, he shook Hiram's hand and went down the road to Virgil's place, whistling, trying to raise up the commotion of nightingales. When he was down a good piece in the full dark, Virgil trudging silently beside him, Sloane turned his head to see the place from where he'd just come, the shadows of his son and family puzzling the warm copper doorway.

Virgil's cabin was not large, but every square inch seemed arranged to achieve a perfection of form. Not one ounce of space was wasted. They pulled up a pair of rockers before a cold fireplace.

"I shouldn't be imposing."

Virgil waved this away and leaned to his little wood stove and poured them both cups of hot lemon water. It was sharp and strong on Sloane's tongue and it recalled the smell of freshly turned land. He searched for a place to set his mug and found a ledge running at shoulder height. As he did so his eyes chanced upon the mantelpiece, where the strangest piece of creation he'd ever laid eyes on rested.

It was a long and slim glass case glutted with entire constellations of sprockets and springs. Every tiny mechanism appeared to be in continuous motion, powered by some invisible strength that operated with the regularity of a river current. The pieces inside shimmered as they sawed and tipped and revolved, creating a kind of lovely illusion of metal afire when they caught the slightest glint of lantern light. Sloane was so taken with the material complexity of the apparatus that it took him a while to make sense of the silver face at the top and the slender hands webbed across it, tapering where they met the besieging numbers.

Virgil followed his gaze and laughed and swiped the clock down so the two old men could have a better look. "My father's. He made a living in Richmond as a watch repairman. But he was a man with a spirit for tinkering and so he saved away every scrap from the shop that he could so that he could build his own perfect clock. Here, let me show you."

Virgil leaned very close and carefully rotated the glass

case so that Sloane could study each aspect, from the base to the top. He allowed a second turn before he smiled and asked him: "Do you see the miracle of it?"

"I didn't see no place for a winding key. There ain't no way to keep it going."

"That's it! He wanted to have a clock that would never run down and never need to be tended nor wound. Something that agreed perfectly with time as how he thought of it. Took him most of his life to learn the tricks. He wasn't any more educated than the average feller and the materials were hard to come by. But he was patient and willing to work at it until he got the principles of the thing down. After that it was only trial and error. Arranging the parts so that as the gears and teeth meshed they spun their answering pieces back, always winding even when it was running to its own end."

They watched the timepiece's roiling guts for a long while before Virgil placed the glass clock back on the mantelpiece and they both drank their hot toddies. Sloane felt the drink having greater effect now, a bone-deep tiredness beginning to take him overall. Virgil saw the weariness in his guest's eyes and rose, saying he would go and set up the spare cot just in case. Then he went to the small backroom smiling as if he'd known all along he would be sheltering a lost soul this night.

Sloane could not resist the desire to lie down, unable even to shuck his boots before his head touched the pillow. A blanket snapped somewhere above so that it billowed like a sail as it settled over him. He would have thanked Virgil if his mind had not been so close to slipping over its final fogged edge into the great colorless warmth of sleep. But he was so tired now. He heard and felt things, but his voice was rusted shut. So even though he seemed blind to the waking world, he knew that Virgil moved quietly to the back of the cabin. He knew these things without seeing them. He dreamed them even before he had slept. And they brought him such great peace.

That night, Sloane traveled the length of his life, but in this dream his days were spent on a strange river enclosed by a gauntlet of dark mountains and the current that bore his canoe was not that of water but air. He carried no paddle nor gear but his way was marked by buoys he could steer to by simply wishing to do so. He could step outside the canoe and walk through the invisible stream and see the levitating trout and small-mouth bass circling his feet and he could hear and understand their fish language and then he would move on and hear the words of men and women and understand them just as well as the fish. Many of these people lived in the empty river with him and their days were spent without strife or discord. But he grew old on the river.

One day death was near and he returned to his canoe to relieve the burden of so much living. He stepped carefully back into the boat, balancing so as not to capsize it, and stretched out with his head propped against the gunwale and watched the slouching mountains pass. Many hundreds of people then came to him, men and women whose faces bore some slight familiarity but whose names were unknown and he realized they were all kin not yet born, men and women he would never know but who had come to see him off on his death just the same. He felt their hands on his face and shoulders, soothing him like mothers easing the delusions of a fevered child. Then they stepped away, receding on the mystic tide that had brought them and there was darkness all about save for a single jewel on the shore. As he drew closer, he could see the spires of reflected light draw down and the object become clearer. The glass clock, now enlarged a hundred times, was the source of the queer light and it shone but did not blind him and he looked on it, going past as the current carried him. He turned to watch it diminish, but even after a very long time, when his eyes saw it only as a speck on the riverbank already gone, the memory of it lived in his mind with the brilliance and stature of a grail.

1918

Nara came down through the high remote trails, chasing the song of robins. Hot and windless, the sky showed brokenly through the latticework of limbs and shade. Even though the trees roofed thick overhead, sunlight and cerulean split through. She came to a clearing and stared up at the lovely emptiness above, expansive and deep as a choir voice. She was lost to it for a moment before the birds cried again, cutting through the sound beneath the sound. She knew she must be getting close now.

The birds had whispered her name at daybreak, the moment when shade mated with sun and the world was born. She'd strained to listen, to see if there was any way it might be a trick of her mind, but the longer she waited the greater the distance between hearing and knowing became, frightening her into wakefulness.

She'd been careful to ease away from Sloane, extract herself from the trap of sleep by degrees so as not to disturb him. She knew how hard it had been for him to rest. Up all hours of the night, silently bearing the pain consuming him from the inside out. Though he didn't complain, she could read it written on the slow and distant smile he forced when she asked if he was feeling well.

Now though, all she could think of was the heat of this day. Her face warmed to the sun and she imagined its print spreading on her skin like a stain the size and shape of a hand. Even with all the years she'd spent in the field working beside her husband, her complexion remained fair and smooth, almost like a girl's. Other women had complimented and tacitly envied her this accident of heredity, but she'd never seen it as anything other than troublesome. The easy burn would be gone within a day, but the browning of regular exposure would never follow. Instead there would be only a gradual fading back to its original pallor.

She heard the weaving music of the birds once more. It came from somewhere high on the ridges the other side of the creek. She was already short of breath from the climb, but the song she'd heard tunneled in her ears and she knew she would be unable to give it up until she was sure whether or not the voice belonged to Kite.

She had never told Sloane nor Hiram that her dead son sometimes came to her. She had tried once, when Sloane had woken from one of his awful nightmares, the ones he used to suffer those years ago when the death was still a new hurt in their lives. There may have been a chance that he would have taken some comfort in knowing that the boy, their sweet child, continued to live in the trees and creeks, changing his form with the seasons. But when the words had come to her mind, she heard how they would sound to him, a man who'd been so hard-ridden by fate. Even if he somehow believed her, he would do so from pity, not really understanding so much as fearing to injure what he would judge as her delusion.

But she knew the things she saw were real. So she did not risk them by making their truth subject to Sloane's tolerance, his disbelief. She had seen enough of that in him already. The way he wrestled with God for the sake of self-spite. That was part of the physical pain he now carried with him. It had to be. Some transformation of his guilt running its course through his life like veins carrying diseased blood through a body. He could never let any of it go. Perhaps he would have grown too lonely without it.

These thoughts weighed. She could hold them up for only so long before they would crush her like a wheel beneath a mountain. There had been a time when she took a strange kind of pride in her ability to suffer without complaint. As if the measure of her misery was in the simple acceptance of her lot as a wife and mother. But she was human too, and it was the human in her that wanted to desert these obligatory sacrifices. She knew she should pray more for her obedience to his will. But sometimes what God asked was too much.

She would admit there were graces. Not many, but some. Like the letter about Hiram. Even when she'd read the military's words, she disbelieved that another of her sons could have been taken from her. That might have been shock, but as the days passed and still she didn't hear a word from him from the other side of death, her suspicion had developed into conviction. She had kept the letter hidden because she feared Sloane discovering it. He would not have the faith she did and she was afraid that hearing of Hiram's death would be more than he could bear. So she guarded it and listened to the silence that answered when she waited for

Hiram to speak to her from wherever Kite was. And the silence took her into its arms so that she never wanted to break its embrace.

She saw an orange flit of color and heard the full, throbbing birdsong, like some profound joy made audible, and she quickened her pace up the path. The coarse briars plucked at her dress as she stepped into an overgrown brake and some places on her skirt caught and rent but she picked her way past and dusted the burrs and brambles away, not letting anything get between her and her boy now.

She remembered Kite when he was just a child and not some miracle of the world beyond this world. When he was locked in the prison of her firstborn's body. Never had there been such a boy like that in either her or Sloane's family. She sometimes wondered if maybe she had favored him too much. But perhaps it wasn't that. Perhaps there was no helping that. What Nara regretted was that Hiram might have seen how much preference she paid to his older brother. Taken it too much to heart and allowed it to form the young man he later became.

She knew her relationship with Kite was what caused the shooting. Not in the literal unfolding of events necessarily, but in the overall spirit in which it transpired. It was simple. She loved Kite too well and God had punished her vanity. But that hadn't been all. It wasn't only the loss of the boy, that was hard enough, but that the agent for her suffering, the man behind the trigger that caused such woe should be the only other person in the world she loved more than prudence and faith. That her heart's secret door should be smashed and violated by the very carpenter who wrought it. That was the true deep kiss of pain.

Even now when she would think of Sloane as a young

man, her head would flood with white light and through that brilliant wound she would remember their first coupling in the narrow cot in the small shotgun house he rented above the sawmill where he was foreman. She would remember the smell of sweat and pine and the soft, textured freckles of sawdust pressed into the dark fleece of the hairs on his chest and arms, and yes, the parts of him that were just questions suggested by the handsome fit of his work clothes, but answers well met in the naked flesh, yes there was that too, the shapely imagination carrying those details back to her like a faithful homing pigeon. She recalled too the clumsy invitation that preceded that warm afternoon of skin and tongues, a fumbling request to share a pot of tea after church, even though she would learn later he had as much use for tea drinking and churchgoing as she did for a carpenter's adz. But he was patient with these illusions of courtship, on the surface at least, and this observation of propriety touched and amused her, made it easier to yield to him when the terror of passing over the serrated edge of sin could not be put off. When he and she clasped, Nara felt herself becoming something more than just a woman, more than an arrangement of tissue and strung nerves. Surely God would forgive her that.

And when Kite was born it was that contentment multiplied. Already there was the house Sloane had built for them, the cabin raised and chinked which would be their home for the rest of their marriage, the little parcel of land that straddled the pleasant creek and forest of mixed hardwoods. She would have never asked him to quit his job as foreman, but he'd sensed her desire to move to their own patch of the world. A place to build up gardens and dreams away from the ritual demands of labor. He understood material accumulation wasn't just uninteresting to her, but an active offense against all that she believed. Other wives might hint at the need for gathered comforts as proof of their husbands' devotion, but Nara hungered for the emptiness and simplicity of a hard life because she knew only a hard life would bring them close to the truth of universal need. She didn't want to separate herself from the adversities of living by collecting adornments and mere paint. So when there was the child, the happiness he brought was complete. There were no possessions to divide the child from the parents and them from each other, and so their seeming want proved to be their surplus. The small, utile world they'd built enclosed them as simply and fully as any myth of Eden.

But all falls are preceded by heights. What was sweet peace when the character of the child was still unformed began to stress and shift as Kite developed a distinct personality. It became clear that the boy and Nara shared certain affinities, exchanged secrets through a magic understanding of slight gestures and moods. Words were crude in comparison to the easy intuitions that passed between them, as if the very air they breathed conveyed the singularity of their interest.

That was when Sloane first took to drinking. Maybe it was not just then, because he'd always favored an evening tot to ease him off to sleep, but the character of the drinking began to change then, just as the character of the child had. It was clear that he loved his son, but father love, Nara knew, is not the same as mother love. It covets far easier. And that's what the love turned to when he saw her bond with the boy. He pined for the lost intimacy of being only two people together, that invention called man and wife. Because when the child was still young it, the love affair, had continued on for a good long while. But when the child became the boy Kite it was forever lost, and the drinking became his way to disguise the heartache and emptiness overtaking him.

She'd noticed the change in Sloane's behavior. It was not flagrant, but it became a tenant in their home, as much as any begrudgingly welcomed guest. And she'd learned to move around it, ignore its insistent presence, but even then she knew there would have to be some form of reparation, some peace offering extended without expecting a due return.

She brushed her long hair forward off her shoulder so that it fanned across her breast. The shadows played coolly along her bent neck. She was pleased to take advantage of this shaded arbor where she waited and watched. She'd lost the robin's trail somehow, but she trusted patience would reward her soon. She felt her dry lips with the back of her hand. She was awfully thirsty. If she didn't find Kite soon, she'd have to leave off for a drink from the creek. But just as she had committed herself to this course of action there the call was again. She set off.

As she trod further up the pathless stretch of woods, she remembered how Hiram seemed born to the rough life she and Sloane had elected. It wasn't that Kite wasn't as much a little boy as any other, but he took to scripture and quiet reflection in a way that Hiram didn't when he was still young. No, for Hiram it was all traipsing after his daddy, wanting to shoot his gun and ride out on that ornery pile of skin and bones Sloane called a mule. As soon as he was big enough to walk on his own two legs there was no keeping him out of the woods, always tearing after bullfrogs and crickets. He pestered her when he first started talking to let him go on with his daddy when he went to hunt a buck. When Sloane one day did drag a brambly racked eight-pointer down from the ridge where he'd shot it, Hiram went right over and bit down as smartly as a hound on its lifeless ear. Sloane had a big laugh over that, but it troubled her in a way she could never bring herself to name.

Even though Kite lived in the regular embrace of his mother, he eventually came to an age when mother love alone wasn't enough. As the elder son, he saw the way new alliances were formed within the family and as he grew they became intolerable, a violation of his male birthright. That was when she'd first realized she would have to give him up. When he too began to follow in his father's shadow. Where before it was Kite and Nara and Sloane and Hiram, now it became a house full of men with a single mother to tend them. Nara had unwittingly created her own banishment, but perhaps that was worth bearing, if only for the sake of her son's truest wish.

So all three were her men, for she already thought of her sons as grown because in that hard world they soon took on the responsibility of adults. There was no easy tenderness to spare when rows needed to be hoed and patches planted. The men took it on themselves to conquer the peace of the garden, to work the land with ferocity and terrible labor.

And she gave Sloane this. She gave him both her boys and his earned bitterness and thought that would be enough. She thought that would expiate her, but she did not realize how deeply the drink had possessed him by then. Not at first. Not until everything had been rendered to him and his way left clear for whatever he might will of them and her, and still he drank himself to black rages and pitiful tears. So it had frightened her, and she said nothing. But in her silence she'd allowed the gun to be loaded. She'd watched Sloane stagger through the night-blackened doorway, careening into the shapeless dark like an overspun globe wobbling free of its axis, hollering for the boys to come on, there were coyotes out there that cried for a killing.

She'd heard the shot come too soon and known that one of the boys was dead. The grief arrived too quick, outdistancing even the news, the order of the universe reversed in those moments that would always mean most. She'd prayed her vain and perverse prayer. She'd wished it Hiram not Kite, and in so doing knew she'd put her dearest one in his grave.

Coming up from the granite ledge, she gained the highest point along the ridge where she could gaze down the entire length of the small valley. The air was slightly cooler and a relief from the humidity that lay on the land like an invisible flood. She breathed it in, filling her lungs and letting the sheen of sweat draw off with the favorable breeze. It was lovely to see the country from here, but there were no birds. She studied the way she'd come, watching for any movement among the trees, but there was nothing to be seen and no company at this height.

"Where have you gone?" she said so quietly the speech died by the time it reached her own ears. Or maybe not. Maybe she'd just imagined that. Maybe her own voice was something already dead in this world. Let the heart speak, then. Let that be enough.

Having no further to climb, she turned back towards the creek bed, hopeful of a new discovery. She believed Kite would find her if she went there. She wanted to believe so, at least. Desertion would be too much to suffer this early in the day, this late in a mother's worried life.

She thought of Hiram now in that terrible place across the surface of the Earth. Would he think of her when he nestled to the gaping dirt? He had written to her a few times in the past few months, describing the muck and slag of war, but she wondered how much could be truly understood from the orderly march of his words across the page. Even when words tried to describe the evil of the world truthfully, there was a strange beauty to loss. That was their great lie. There were places though between the language that said more. She hadn't imagined that. It was as real as the silence between the mountains and sky.

Hiram had once written that he renounced God because why should God ask so many of his sons to die for him. What kind of father would ask such things? And that was how she knew he wasn't dead now, would never be killed by something as fickle as war because he lived in the closed heart of his own suffering. Such suffering was deep and vindictive and would never give him up until he'd accepted it, but he would never do that, because Hiram carried man blood and man blood has an awful innocence that leaves it blind to the truth of its affinity.

She heard the robin song again, but it had become solitary and low and tentative, a sad poem in the brush. Her feet stilled on the trail. She did not know why she paused, but some vague suspicion held her, reaching through the skin to lay its cold finger to her core. But she had to go on and she did.

The creek shimmered. Nothing visible on it but time and sun. Still, stock-still, she heard the robin's song rising from beneath the water, as ungarbled as if it passed through free air. She slipped her shoes from her feet and felt the cool water grasp her with gentleness as she stepped into a mirrored pool.

Again. *Again*, that favorite word of hers. *Again*.

The robin answered and she recognized then the call down to its nest. The sound beneath the sound. The place where breath begins and ends. The soles of her feet passed over the sandy bottom as smoothly as if it were made of glass. She dipped her face into the water, letting it pull on her. Her mind at work now, a shrewd conjurer, thinking while she still could, finding a path to regret.

A sky like this, reflected in water, something so emptied of form and shape, reminded her of a rifle shot. Under a sky like this it all comes to pass.

She put her hands in the water and knotted her skirts. Then she began to fill the small pocket she'd made with stones from the creek, counting them as you would all the lambs of men when sheep would not do, reaching out somewhere beyond the outer boundary of sleep. The weight drew her down with an invitation to peace, a place never to be discovered, defended, or claimed. A place where none wished to breathe. Into that slow country she went.

Acknowledgments

My special thanks to Ron Earl Phillips and everyone at Shotgun Honey for giving this book a second life. As before, this book is because of A., E., and I.

Portions of this novel appeared previously in *Night Train* and *Wrong Tree Review*

I would like to thank Rachel Harper and Crystal Wilkinson for their encouragement and insight—proof that fine writers are so often fine people. To Robin Lippincott my greatest gratitude for being a believer in this book when that was what was needed most. That and a true friend, too.

CHARLES DODD WHITE is the recipient of the Thomas and Lillie D. Chaffin Award for excellence in Appalachian Literature, the Appalachian Book of the Year award in fiction, a Jean Ritchie Fellowship from Lincoln Memorial University, and an individual artist's grant from the North Carolina Arts Council. His novels are *HOW FIRE RUNS* (A Fall 2020 SIBA Okra Pick, IPPY GOLD MEDAL for Best Fiction in the South), *IN THE HOUSE OF WILDERNESS* (2018), *A SHELTER OF OTHERS* (2014), *LAMBS OF MEN* (2010), and the story collection, *SINNERS OF SANCTION COUNTY* (2011). He has also edited the anthologies, *DEGREES OF ELEVATION* (2010) and *APPALACHIA NOW* (2015). His essay collection, *A YEAR WITHOUT MONTHS*, was published by West Virginia University Press in 2022. He teaches English at Pellissippi State Community College in Knoxville, Tennessee.

COMING SOON
FROM
SHOTGUN HONEY BOOKS

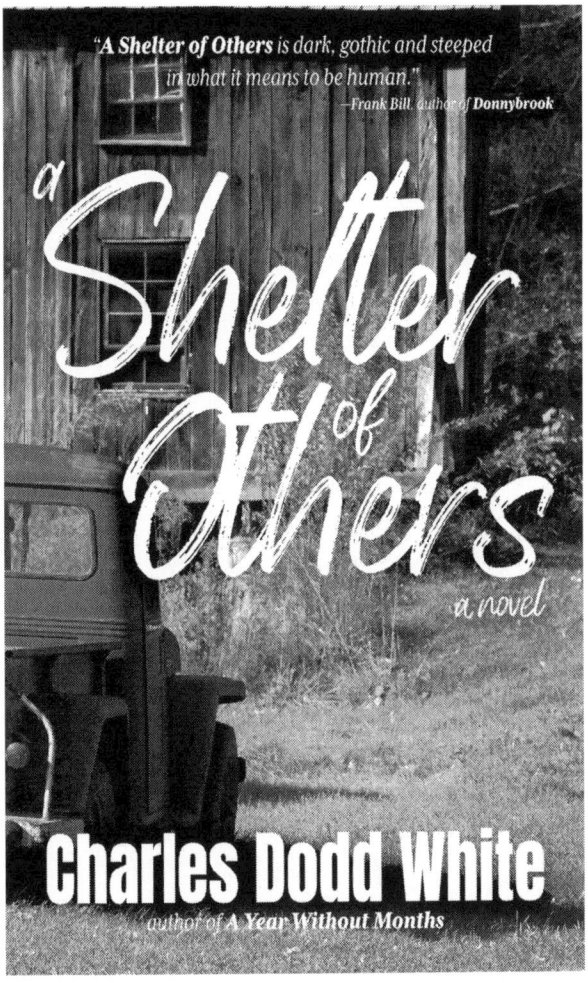

"*A Shelter of Others* is dark, gothic and steeped in what it means to be human."
—Frank Bill, author of *Donnybrook*

A Shelter of Others
a novel

Charles Dodd White
author of *A Year Without Months*

A Shelter of Others
by Charles Dodd White
DECEMBER 2022

SHOTGUN HONEY
2012 • 2022

CELEBRATING 10 YEARS OF
FICTION WITH A KICK

THE ROAD IS JUST BEGINNING
shotgunhoneybooks.com

Made in the USA
Columbia, SC
24 October 2024